The Art of the Imperfect
a crime mystery set in Scarborough
Kate Evans

'The only real mistake you can make as a counsellor is to die.'
Gestalt Counselling in Action, Petruska Clarkson,
Sage Publications, London, Newbury Park, New Delhi, 1989, p. 91.

Chapter 1

There's footsteps. Are they inside? Or outside? Of the building? Of her head? Are they coming to get her?

Hannah rouses herself just enough to remember something from a self-defence for women class she took once when those things were fashionable. Keys. She has keys. Hold them between your fingers and jab the sharp ends into your attacker's eyes. She can do this. *Look for your keys, Hannah. Where are they? I've lost them.* They should be in her bag. Maybe she dropped them and they already have them. Accomplices are at this very moment on their way to her parents' home to kill them.

Something is rising up her throat. It tastes like panic. Like a scream. Like bile. No, here are her keys, in her pocket. She holds them tightly, the warm metal biting into her fingers. She's cold, and stiff, from sitting on the floor. Better to be standing. She begins to lever herself upright, leaning into the corner where door jamb meets wall. She can smell damp.

Right, I'm ready for you now. She tenses her muscles. More footsteps. *Where are they? Upstairs? Coming through the back? Where? Behind her?* Bang, bang, bang. There's bells. *The fire alarm? They've started a fire?*

She has to get out. She reaches behind her and pulls at the door handle; it won't turn, they've tied it shut. No, no, she's turning it the wrong way and there's the Yale to contend with. *Come on, Hannah!* She scrabbles at the lock and finally drags the heavy wooden barrier open. Cold air tumbles into her. *Who? What?* They're there on the doorstep. Expletives catapult through her brain. She thinks she screams loud enough for someone in the Ramsdale pub to hear and come and help. She doesn't. Her shoulder and arm are painfully fused to the door frame. She is paralysed waiting for the blow which must surely come.

'Ms Poole?'

'You know my name?' she squeaks, registering how unattractive she sounds.

'You phoned in? DC Harriet Shilling and PC Trevor Trench.'

Hannah can see now; the shapes are becoming human. Both taller than her, though that wouldn't be hard. The woman is wearing a brown suede jacket over brown slacks, her blonde hair gripped back. The man is broad in his fluorescent yellow jacket with its plethora of implements and devices hanging off, like he is in some weird game of Buckaroo.

The woman is in charge, she ascertains where she needs to go and tells Trev to wait. Trev nods. He stands there in the centre of the path. *Is he protecting me or stopping me from running away?* The chill is seeping into her and a smog of tiredness descends; if she weren't leaning against something, she would fall. She can hear the sounds of the street penetrating the hedge which surrounds the Centre; cars braking for the junction and then accelerating away, a dog's nose sniffs in at the open iron gate and 'Rory' is called to come on. Finally, unable to bear the silence between them, Hannah mentions how cold the weather's got. Trev nods. A couple of young women trip past on what sound like very high heels. A car blares its horn. Hannah is beginning to shiver.

'Right, then.' DC Shilling's bright voice makes Hannah jump. 'We've got to secure the scene, Trev, and call in the CSI.' Trev nods and then turns away to begin to report something into the radio on his shoulder. Hannah is surprised he can be so articulate.

'Ms Poole, if you could come with me?' It sounds like a request, only DC Shilling has her hand firmly, if gently, on Hannah's shoulder and her hold brooks no argument. Hannah is guided to the police car parked outside the gate and into its back seat. It smells of cleaning fluid, but she is glad of the warmth. The policewoman gets out a pen and notepad from an inside pocket. 'Now, can you tell me what happened, please, Ms Poole?'

Hannah begins to explain how she'd gone to the library at the Scarborough Centre for Therapy Excellence to check some references for her essay.

'On a Sunday?'

'It's due in tomorrow.'

'You're training here?'

'Yes, to be a counsellor.' She tries to restart her tale and DC Shilling interrupts again, asking where the library is. 'Downstairs.'

'So why did you go upstairs, Ms Poole?'

She can't say why exactly, a feeling. Then, to her embarrassment, Hannah finds she is sobbing and hot watery lines score down her frozen face. Her words become completely obscured by her efforts to breathe and cry at the same time.

'It's OK, Ms Poole, here.' DC Shilling hands over a couple of tissues. A strand of white-blonde hair has escaped from its clips, softening the tautness of her feverishly blushered cheekbones. 'So you have no idea whether Dr Themis Greene was in the building when you first arrived? Or indeed whether there was anyone else in the building?'

'I'm sorry?' Hannah manages to whisper as she tries to stem the insistent dribble of tears.

'Well,' DC Shilling looks past her, 'it's a big building. Victorian.' She sighs quietly. 'The Sitwells lived next door, you know.'

'The who?' Hannah sniffs. She feels cocooned, safe, leans back against the seat and closes her gritty eyes.

'Writers? Twentieth century? Edith? Poetry?'

'Lawrence would know,' Hannah says sleepily.

There's a pause and then a knock at the window by Hannah's side makes her start. DC Shilling is all action again. She unlocks the car door — Hannah had not realised she had been locked in and this gives her another little shock — and propels Hannah out onto the street.

Away from her cosy nest Hannah sees that things have been happening: blue and white police tape has appeared, along with more officers and people in white paper over-alls carrying what look like toolboxes. She meets a man on the front path. Black, she notes immediately; she wouldn't normally do so if she were back home in London, but this is Scarborough. He is lean, his hair cut back to the skull, his dark eyes appraise her from behind red-framed glasses. And he's wearing, can it be? A duffle coat? It gives him the air of an emaciated Paddington Bear. She realises this is not an accidental encounter as he introduces himself as Detective Sergeant Theo Akande. She wants to ask him how on earth he got to be a detective sergeant in Scarborough, but he's posing the questions. His accent pins him to the map, somewhere in the posh end of Birmingham. Not like hers: unpinned, twittering, middle class.

She has to go through it all again. The smog is back, she's not even sure if she is telling the same story this time around. *What happens if I get it a bit wrong? Will they suspect me?*

DS Akande doesn't immediately respond when she's finished. Eventually he asks her the question she cannot answer: why did she go upstairs? Maybe there was a light, she says tentatively, from under one of the doors.

'And Dr Greene was dead when you entered the room?'

She feels a sick panic; had she been? An image comes to mind, a large rag doll, its body bowed over, dark hair a neat, sleek curtain across the face. The sharp smell of ammonia. She takes a step forward and gently prods at the jacket-clad shoulder. The rag doll rolls a little, so that she is looking into the profile of a face, a very human face, covered in damson-coloured oily paint. She recognises the features: she has seen them a hundred times on textbook covers and in journals, only the face had been oval, the skin peachy smooth, not this hideously caved-in grey.

'Ms Poole, was she dead?'

She nods and screeches, 'Yes, yes.' So why does she see an animated, talking face? It must come from watching Dr Greene giving a recorded conference lecture. She wasn't alive when Hannah first entered that, that human abattoir. *Was she?*

8

'Did you touch her?'

'I don't think so.' For the first time she notices drying brown stains on the cuffs and skirt of her coat. She brings her hand up to her mouth to cover her gag and an unsavoury odour makes her stomach lurch uneasily. She clamps her teeth.

Akande is watching her intently. She shakes from her chilled insides, even as her skin catches alight. He calls over a tall, thin, white-paper-suited man who performs a strange kind of manicure. Akande says she'll have to come down to the station the next day to give her prints and make a statement. They need her clothes.

'What, now? Here?'

It's true, sometimes a smile can transform a face: he suddenly looks friendly, like a good mate, like he'd be a good laugh even. No, they will take her home and retrieve them from her there.

'I can go home?' she whispers; rather pathetically, she realises.

He nods. Harry will go with her. She wonders who Harry is, until DC Shilling is once again guiding her to the police car and into the back seat.

It's not a long drive to her parents' home on Sea View Lane and they are nearly there before Hannah begins to wonder what on earth she is going to tell her mum and dad. All she wants to do is have a shower and dig herself a cave in the duvet and sleep, sleep for a thousand years. Harry stops outside the house and Hannah wants to stay where she is, snooze there; she thinks briefly about asking the policewoman if that would be allowed. Then she injects some fuse wire into her legs and spine, and walks as steadily as she can manage into the house, Harry following.

She glances briefly at the hall grandfather clock: its ridiculously over-ornate gold-coloured hands tell her she's only been away for maybe two hours. It feels like months have passed. She can hear the TV from the snug and knows her mother will be in there, a glass of sherry (probably her third or fourth) on the spindly-legged dark-wood occasional table by her side. As she ascends the stairs — Harry, silent and dogged on her heels — she hears her father coughing in his office. She tiptoes quietly past and up the second flight to the spare (her temporary) bedroom in the roof.

Squares of dark-violet sky punched with ice are visible through the skylights. They remind Hannah of the expanse of sea at the bottom of the cliffs, at the edge of the garden. She shuts them out, pulling down the blinds. DC Shilling is waiting. Hannah goes into the ensuite and strips, pulling a towel around her, she doesn't want to put on her Ted Baker kimono until she's scrubbed herself clean.

She returns to the bedroom. The other woman unbends from examining the few photos — of Lawrence in his kitchen and of Rickie, Steff and herself at a club — which are stuck into a flower-shaped stand on the desk. Hannah wonders what else she has been going through, noticing her hands have acquired latex gloves. The police officer produces a bag for the clothes, which she then tapes shut. She looks like she might be about to start questioning again, but Hannah wants her gone. She asks her sharply if she can find her own way out. DC Shilling inclines her head and goes.

Hannah feels all the fire and venom leave her, she thinks of merely collapsing into bed, maybe on waking she will find that none of this has happened. But no, she's only too clear about what has occurred and she needs to scour it all away. She turns on the radio, music blares out, a 'golden oldie', she turns up the volume, then turns it down, remembering her father in his office on the floor below. She hums to herself, 'Mmm mmm, gonna get better, mmm, mmm, mmm, gonna get better,' as she showers, allowing the hot water to pound onto her head and shoulders. Finally she feels less soiled. She gives her hair a perfunctory once-over with the dryer. It will be a nest in the morning. She doesn't care. She will sort it out then. *Everything will be fine once more in the morning,* she thinks as she burrows deeply into bed and falls asleep.

Chapter 2

The vast Victorian graveyard which cuts a green swathe through the north side of Scarborough borders the back of the police station. The offices on the second and third floor look down on an ordered, if overgrown, patterning of grass, hebe and rhododendron bushes, between curved pathways and grey monuments, all contained within a ten-foot-high brick wall. Theo takes the short walk down a snicket, through a wrought-iron gate and into the cemetery to where the renovated tiled mausoleum offers shelter from the damp air. It's here he finds Suze smoking a stringy roll-up. She carefully puts it out and away into her baccy tin as he sits next to her, then she wraps her painfully red, crooked hand joints into the thick, dark-green knitted shawl she is wearing. It must be a good day because her crutches lean up against the bench. Theo can smell the usual mix of Golden Virginia and peppermint emanating from her narrow, hunched shoulders. It reminds him of a couple of his unmarried aunts who were always a soft touch for sweets or money.

'Taking a break, Sarge?'

He nods. The atmosphere in here is calm, unlike the frenetic, even manic, energy of the incident room. It feels almost homely, despite their mingled breath condensing on the ceramic-covered walls decorated with delicately painted posies of forget-me-nots and ferns.

'It's a big case; everyone is talking about it,' Suze continues.

'What are they saying?'

'Oh, you know.' Suze takes in all the gossip as secretary to the DI, but rarely gives it out unless it's useful.

'Any bets being taken yet on whether I'll make a fool of myself? I know some of them are waiting for that.' He's working on finding ways to blend in, like not asking for a cob at lunchtime.

Suze smiles, a warm curve of the lips which reaches her navy eyes. 'You won't though, Sarge, you're doing OK.'

'Thanks for the vote of confidence, only there's still so much I don't know about this place.'

'What's there to know? Small town, petty grievances, petty criminals, everyone with their neb in each other's business.' And Suze Irvine, née Pritchard, coming from one of the sprawling Old Town fishing families and married into the amusements' king clan, knows all the intricate interweaving of alliances and relationships. 'But this comes from out of town, doesn't it? Dr Greene wasn't from around here. She hardly landed long enough to get her toenails wet.'

'Did you come across her when she was director of the Centre?'

'No, all that therapy stuff, it's another world; besides it's south side.'

'Don't you know anyone that end?'

'A few, mainly girls I went to school with who've moved ova.'

'Well, Dr Greene might be from elsewhere, but her killer could well be from the town. The last person who saw her was one of her clients.'

'Makes sense that it's one of the nutters.'

Theo has heard this a number of times now and still hasn't found the right response, one which won't open him up too much, he knows how vulnerable to attack he already is. 'I wouldn't say he's mad.'

'Then what's he seeing a psychotherapist for? There was that case, wasn't there, not so long ago, a schizo with a knife? If they don't get their medicine they don't know what they're doing.'

'He's not schizophrenic, just been a bit depressed.'

Suze makes a noise which suggests she doesn't think this is a good enough reason to seek help.

'What about the woman who found the body?' Suze doesn't have to add, 'Another outsider' and, therefore, a candidate for suspicion; it comes through in her tone. Even though Stan Poole had been in the town for over ten years, is retired editor of its paper, this doesn't make him, or his daughter (who'd never lived in the town), a local.

'I don't think so. On first inspection there wasn't enough blood on her. Forensics should tell us more. And it's unlikely she'd have called the police if she'd been the killer.' *Unlikely, though not unheard of.* Theo remembers the petite Hannah Poole with her ferociously flattened, fiercely burgundy-tinted hair. She had been unsettlingly obscure at times in making her statements. *Why had she gone upstairs and into the room? Had she done anything to the body?* 'Nothing's clear as yet.' Theo feels like he's been swimming in very murky water. Apart from the clients, there's Dr Greene's personal relationships, which have been cause of much debate, some of it too raucous and scathing for Theo to feel comfortable. Dr Greene had a conventional marriage in 1968 at the age of twenty-six to an academic who founded a now-prestigious journal where she had her first publishing success. This lasted a prodigious thirty years and was ended, according to the ex-husband, amicably due to 'growing philosophical differences'. Then Dr Greene had a four-year relationship with a woman called Eve, who is proving hard to find, before having a civil partnership with Penny almost as soon as that became possible. In addition, Theo has heard suggestions of jealous colleagues and money that's turned up in an Antiguan bank account.

'Guess the DI is putting the pressure on, he doesn't like unsolved murders in his dredge.' It's not a guess, but a gentle warning from someone who knows her boss well and has worked at the station since leaving school. And, no doubt, her husband's fitted the DI's gas central heating and her eight-year-old daughter plays with the DI's children. DI Hoyle is an absent SIO, at the moment. Theo is learning that his superior is never one to stretch himself and is intent on rolling as unperturbed as possible towards retirement. Currently, however, the DI is also having a phased return to work after a heart op. There's talk of bringing in another Senior Investigating Officer. Meanwhile Theo is taking the strain. 'There's one girl I know from the south side, Aurora

Sharma as was, now Aurora Harris,' Suze continues like she's saying something very inconsequential. Theo knows not to hurry her. 'Her parents were GPs over there, they've retired to Cornwall. Aurora and I met at a drama club. Her bloke, Max, hails from Malton, he's got his own design company. She's a solicitor, a family one, working in York. They're expecting their first child soon. Aurora was at school with Eve Cooper, and helped her out later on with something messy to do with a divorce.'

Theo is alert: Eve Cooper, the elusive lover in the middle. 'And Dr Greene was involved?'

'I wouldn't know, Aurora's not one to discuss someone else's tragedy with me. When we see each other it's usually to go to the theatre or see some film.' Suze collects her crutches and stands up, her face on a level with the seated Theo's. She gives him an encouraging grin and suggests they both should be getting back. As he adjusts his pace to her slower one, he asks her whether she ever thought of becoming a police officer.

'What, the force's first immobile response unit? I don't think they're quite ready for that.' She laughs when Theo mentions the Disability Discrimination Act. 'How sweet and new to here you are. Anyway,' her thick eyebrows draw together, 'I wouldn't want to be a token. Would you?'

He thinks she probably knows how much of a token he is and that's why she allows him into her haven when others have been curtly barred. He is grateful for her kindness.

'Right.' She pauses at the back entrance. 'Ready to get back onto the swell?'

He nods and pushes the door open for them both.

Chapter 3

Aurora is sitting on her sofa — though she'd rather be lying down — her swollen ankles resting on the glass coffee table, and the baby, her baby, is headbutting her bladder and kicking her lungs. All around is devastation: dirty mugs and even a couple of used plates; newspapers; magazines; bills and official letters which need looking at and no doubt actioning; various consoles and games boxes abandoned by Max. Her heels are making sweaty rings on the top already furred with dust and spills. Her briefcase has burst open where she dropped it, papers spilling out. She can smell last night's Chinese takeaway mingling with the moist odour coming from her own flesh. *It's not meant to be like this.* She wants to scream but can't even raise the energy for that; all that comes out is a dry sob. She rests her hot forehead onto her aching hands. *Why didn't Mum tell me? She must have known.*

The next minute Max is crashing into the room. Or it feels like only a minute. She checks her watch: it's been forty-five minutes. He tells her she looks awful, hasn't she had a shower? And then quickly says that even so he still loves her, kissing her firmly on the mouth. He starts pulling off his fuchsia-coloured silk tie from his stout neck and unbuttoning his lavender shirt, his face pink under his white-blonde thatch. He's talking about his day, he's closed a good deal on some marketing campaign and website design project and excited words cascade out of him. She closes her eyes. *Won't you please be quiet?* Then his voice, suddenly sharpened, jerks her awake. 'Want anything?'

She surveys the mess around her. 'For this to be cleared up, for the house to be clean, not to feel like an elephant, not to be smelly and, oh Christ, I want to sleep,' she wails.

His pale-blue eyes blink at her. 'I meant, did you want a cup of tea or something?' She shakes her head, sniffing ineffectually as the tears flow. She's never cried so much in her life; it's as if the amniotic fluid is flooding out of her eyes. Max grumphs, then he comes over and strokes her shoulder. He tells her to go upstairs, have a shower, have a lie-down, he'll sort out in here and cook them something to eat. His culinary abilities haven't stretched much further than scrambled eggs since she first met him; however, Aurora knows she is too tired to do anything herself. She protests weakly that the bathroom also needs a clean. Another grumph. 'It's not that bad, Aurora, just ignore it for now and I'll organise a cleaner tomorrow. Old Mrs Poole next door has someone. It'll be alright, pet,' he finishes gently. As she makes her slow and awkward way off the sofa and to the door he suggests maybe she should think about stopping work.

This elicits another wail which she tries to bring under control. 'I said I'd work until the last moment.'

She expects him to argue his point; instead he says quietly, 'I think this is the last moment, Aurora, I think it is time.' He adds in a more cajoling tone, 'Your boss'll be fine about it, she's had three of her own. She said you could decide when was right for you.'

She says no as she leaves the room, though it's a weary no and as she negotiates the stairs and into the shower, the idea of stopping work begins to take root. Her whole body is aching. The pain in her neck rolls away with the shower water as she thinks about not having to do the daily train commute, or sit at a desk, or stay awake through case conferences and in front of irate clients. *I've had enough. Yes, Mum may have done her last surgery hours before her waters broke, but I have had enough.*

Remarkably Max has managed to make quite a good job of tidying the sitting room and of making a macaroni cheese. And after they've eaten and he's washed up he insists on rubbing oil into her feet and lower legs. The massaging sends her back to sleep, so it is Max who answers the call on her mobile from Eve Cooper, responding that Aurora can't speak right now but will ring back tomorrow.

However, the next morning that undertaking is forgotten and not transmitted to Aurora. She sleeps until midday, by which time Max has arranged for a cleaner to come. Aurora decides it's best to stay in bed rather than risk becoming a nag to the woman who has arrived in her little van with 'Rose Short: gardening, cleaning, personal care' emblazoned on the side. Aurora goes through some of her work emails on her laptop, not fully concentrating, until she is released into a pristine house and best of all a bleached bathroom. She takes her time to bathe and moisturise her tawny skin, which has lost its darker tones during the winter; and condition her jet hair so that it shines once more. When she was younger it fell straight to her waist to please her father, and on holidays with her cousins from her Indian side they would oil and braid and coil it as they did their own. These days she has a practical bob, but she misses having someone else make a fuss of it. She even has time to paint her fingernails and so is feeling almost like her old self when the front doorbell rings. She opens the door to a blonde woman and a lithe black man in a duffle coat and red-rimmed glasses. She invites DC Harry Shilling and DS Theo Akande in, offers them tea, which they refuse, and then sits down with them in the lounge, taking the sofa while they take the two easy chairs. They are looking for Eve Cooper. Aurora remembers the mousy little girl, daughter of a local farmer, who grew into an unconfident adult, married too young another farmer, was an unhappy mother of two boys born in quick succession and then became another person on finding Dr Themis Greene.

'How did they meet?' asks the DS. Harry is apparently there just to take notes.

'She started having therapy with her.'

'Dr Greene was her psychotherapist?'

'Yes. It was after the birth of Eve's second child; she was really down. She was always down, but because it was after childbirth they said it might be post-natal depression, so she was referred to Dr Greene. Or maybe her father found her for her: I know she had to go private and I'm pretty sure her father paid. Reluctantly no doubt, knowing him.'

'So she changed?'

'Yes, blossomed. Started looking after herself more, going to the hairdresser, getting nice clothes, those sort of long, hippy-type skirts and dresses. They weren't really in fashion, though she looked nice in them. And speaking her mind more. Then she upped and left, her sons, her husband, the farm; all of a sudden she was gone.'

'With Dr Greene?'

She nods. 'To Jersey. Dr Greene already had her place out there. Those poor boys, they've never forgiven their mother.'

'And did Eve keep in contact with you?'

'Not exactly.' Aurora hesitates: though technically Eve was never her client, she feels some loyalty to her. The DS is waiting, his face neutral. Finally Aurora says, 'She divorced her first husband and because she'd done the leaving, got pretty much nothing. But she did have an inheritance which was hers. However, she apparently handed it all over to Dr Greene. It went into buying a holiday cottage which Dr Greene is sole owner of and rents out. When things began to go badly between them, Eve contacted me. She told me they'd got married, which, of course, was nonsense: it was some new-agey ceremony, it had no legal status. They were three years too early for civil partnerships. So she was losing the person she still called the love of her life, and she had no money. She'd never considered what would happen if things didn't work out, she'd never seen it as a possibility. I got the impression Dr Greene wielded all the power. There wasn't much I could help Eve with. She'd given all her money away; what she'd earned had gone to Dr Greene. Eve didn't have any rights to anything when she was eventually turfed out. I believe Dr Greene changed the locks on the house. It was awful for Eve, she was destroyed.'

'This was when Penny came on the scene?'

'I'm not sure if there was an overlap exactly. Initially it didn't seem to be about another person, another woman; more Dr Greene getting, I don't know, bored maybe? I really wasn't privy to all the ins and outs.'

'Do you know where Eve is now?'

Aurora has an address from years back, but it turns out to be the one Theo has already checked and found Eve gone from some years before, leaving no trace of where she was headed.

He asks whether Aurora knows anything else about Dr Greene or Eve Cooper, and she says she doesn't. He hands her his card and says to get in touch if anything occurs to her. He's about to leave and Harry is already packing away her notebook when Theo pauses and resettles himself back into his chair. 'Did you ever meet Dr Greene?'

'Only the once. Eve invited me and Max out for a meal with them at some fancy restaurant in York.'

'What was she like, Dr Greene?'

Aurora considers this, tries to muster up some memory of the evening. It couldn't have been awful or it would have stuck with her. 'She was charming, amusing, beautiful in a way, very chiselled face, tall, imposing, wore a designer trouser suit — and gold, I recall expensive gold jewellery. She was a bit, a bit,' she searches and comes up with, 'oily?' Is that disappointment in Akande's features? Had he expected something more? Something other? She shrugs to show she has nothing to add. He thanks her for her time and exits the house. Aurora is slightly unsettled: has she said too much, or too little? Then tiredness overcomes her, she numbly settles back onto the sofa and turns on the radio, half-listening as documentaries dissolve into news as she drifts in and out of slumbering. It is only much later in the evening when she mentions Akande's visit and Max remembers Eve's phone call. He is ghoulishly intrigued: does Aurora think Eve could have done it? She sees again the wan teenager and thinks not, and then recalls Eve's assertiveness and how brittle that seemed. 'Dr Greene certainly did enough to make her angry for a long, long time,' she concludes.

She does call Eve the next morning and leaves a message before, with some misgivings, passing the details on to Akande. Eve does not phone back and when Aurora tries again there's a message saying the number is no longer in use.

Chapter 4

Pink-tinged morning mists begin to rise off the fields, revealing flat, mud-mired earth and thin lines of skeletal trees stretching out to where the Wolds create their sudden flinty escarpment. Hannah gazes out of the window for a while as the train rattles along, apparently pleased at its mediocre speed. She is mesmerised by the wheeling charcoal shapes of birds ascending, forming into a comma and then falling away again, only to gather themselves again for the next configuration. How long would they carry on with these strange acrobatics? Are they native or migrating somewhere? She shakes herself: *do I care?*

She pulls her woollen jacket closer around her shoulders; the weak sun is catching the glimmers of the frost still lingering on the stubble and grass. Refocusing she sees herself in the glass. Despite her efforts at straightening, her hair has frizzed and it also needs re-tinting. She hasn't trusted it to a Scarborough hairdresser, but now she has the chance to get it done properly. Steff commented on a photo Hannah posted on Facebook about liking the 'new natural look'. Hannah doesn't think it was a compliment. She touches her cheeks; maybe she should get a facial too, that raw north-east wind has taken its toll. She turns away.

Lawrence will be amazed she caught this early train when he prophesied that she'd never manage it. She takes out her phone ready to text him, only she is dragged back into the reason for her premature start. The dream. She's in a house, an abandoned house. In her waking life it is not familiar to her, but in her dream she knows it well. Two men have come through the back door and they are looking for her; they will do her a lot of harm. In the dream Hannah tries to scream, to yell out for her parents, who could come and save her, only she cannot make any sound. Now Hannah feels that same surge of panic and tension up through her throat. She closes her eyes and swallows hard. Oh, but there is no-one to save her. *Then I'd better save myself,* she tells herself severely and, opening her eyes, she turns back to her phone. It's hardly surprising that she's had a

20

nightmare since the, the, 'incident' her mind provides helpfully, adding the quote marks as well.

The one good thing is that it has allowed her some escape. Frederick Gough had texted on the Monday to say that given the sad demise of Dr Themis Greene, a great loss to the psychotherapy world and a dear friend, he was cancelling training for a week. They would make the hours up by having less time off at Easter. *Yeah, right,* Hannah had thought, *as if the police would have let him into the building.* However, she had been relieved. She could get away from that awful place. Get away from her parents, her father's angry 'Why didn't you tell me, a big story like that?' And his furious look when she had flung back, 'Dad, they've got someone else to cover it.' Luckily she didn't add, 'Someone younger and anyway you aren't editor any more.' Get away from everyone and get back to her real life, her real friends. She could be there on Friday, Lawrence's birthday. She has some plans to make it a special day for him, though she knows he will have most of it organised by now and it will include entertaining people, with a myriad of delicacies he's already preparing. She would have gone straight away, only there was the small matter of the police and the statement; perhaps it was going through it all again with Harry that had brought on the nightmare. *Yes, that must be it.*

She looks at her phone. There's finally a response from Rickie; for someone whose phone is a permanent appendage, he takes an awful long time to reply. He's given the name of a familiar bar and a time when he will be there tomorrow evening. It's an invitation of sorts. She forwards it to Steff, though knows she will already have been told. 'So looking forward to seeing you guys,' she types, her fingers unusually stiff and uncooperative. The train winds and clatters on into York, picking up at its one stop along the way suited commuters and schoolchildren trying to be cool in their expensive turquoise uniforms. The smell of a bacon butty reaches Hannah's end of the carriage, making her regret her lack of breakfast.

At York she has enough time to buy a coffee and a pastry along with 'Chat', 'Heat' and 'Hello'. On the London train, she settles herself with her refreshments ready to enjoy her magazines. She begins to page through, only she can't latch onto anything; not even the pages of fashion can spark an interest. Perhaps Lawrence is right to scoff at her reading matter. She has some kind of historical romance that she picked off her mother's bookshelf in her bag. It looks like it's never been opened and she can't find the impetus to change that. She dozes, half-aware that the train is halting for stations. It starts over, she is in an abandoned house, there are intruders at the back door, no, not this again, she yanks herself out of sleep, her head snapping painfully backwards. Her shoulders are aching. She opens the book at random to give the appearance of reading: no-one must suspect how crazy she is feeling. Her thoughts are tripping over themselves: *bad Hannah, stupid girl, evil child. Wicked, wicked, wicked.* There's Dr Greene's crushed-in face, turning towards her, grinning at her. Hannah's fury quivers through her. *Focus, Hannah, on the page in front of you, the neat, ordered line of words, make sense of them, they will banish the madness. And most of all, don't let anyone see what's really going on for you.*

At last the brown countryside is beginning to change into suburban sprawl. She recognises the North Circular and then Alexandra Palace. She stretches and feels some of the tension slip away. There's a text on the phone; she opens it eagerly. 'Hello Hannah, I thought we had a session yesterday evening? Best wishes Izzie Bourne.' *Shit,* she had completely forgotten, that's another therapy hour she'll have to make up. And, she suddenly realises, that's £40 wasted. *Shit.* She wonders if Izzie would let her off the money if she claims distress following 'The Incident'.

Lawrence had been as horrified as she when she had discovered the weekly therapy stipulation for the course. Plus she had to do extra because she had somehow avoided doing more than a few weeks during her previous counselling training, which confession had brought a great deal of tut-tutting from

Fred. It had felt like she'd been handed down a life sentence. It still does. Not that there is anything wrong with Izzie: she's quite a pleasant woman, even if she could do a bit more with some judicial use of foundation. It's just that Hannah can't ever think of anything to say to her. In addition, in Hannah's opinion, Izzie seems overly interested in her childhood and relationships with her parents and other family members. 'Fine,' is all Hannah could think to say. 'Everything was and is fine.'

'And how would you describe your parents?' Izzie pushed after a moment's silence.

'Oh, you know, mostly harmless,' Hannah said, grinning. Izzie didn't appear to get the joke, so Hannah began to explain it.

'Yes, I have read Douglas Adams,' Izzie said rather stiffly. No sense of humour, then, Hannah noted.

'And Lawrence?' Izzie had said. 'He seems to loom large in your life?' Well, of course, he does: her landlord, her friend, her saviour. She hadn't said the last to Izzie, though she thinks now that it's true. She had failed at her journalism course, failed at numerous jobs, failed to make much of a life for herself in London, was unemployed, homeless and on the point of having to move back in with her parents, when he stepped in. As a favour to her father, who had been his mentor when Lawrence had started out as a young reporter in the regions. She knew that. Though she was fairly certain he hadn't stuck around until now just for that. The train begins its final entry into the metropolis through an unremitting succession of tunnels. Hannah's ears pop. She is descending into an underworld, mole-like. She has a sudden desire to scurry back to the infinite horizons provided by the sea and the sky of Scarborough. How strange. She dismisses it all with thoughts of Lawrence. He had promised to be at home for her arrival. He will have prepared for her a sumptuous pizza and salad. Hannah licks her lips: it will be such a treat after her mother's lacklustre attempts at meals. Lawrence may even have a rosé in the fridge and have baked scones for afternoon tea. He will have put flowers in her bedroom. It will be like old times. He will be curious about her experiences as he always is. Though it's his solid presence she has missed most. Not an overly demonstrative man, nevertheless she knows he will greet her with an all-enveloping hug into which she will be able to just let go of it all, of everything. She smiles ridiculously, extravagantly.

****

'You look like death,' Lawrence says as she enters the kitchen. It's the morning after her big night out with Rickie and Steff.

'Thanks.' She's given up with her hair and she knows from her glance in the mirror her eyes are more red than hazel and her face looks like it's been created by some kid with over-used putty. She's still in her pyjamas and has on a dressing gown, a cast-off from Lawrence, which is far too big for her but is too comfortable to give up on. She refuses a cooked breakfast and accepts coffee and toast with honey, even though her stomach growls at the thought and the little hammers in her head are giving her no peace.

'How's Rick-the-Dick?'

'He's fine, we had a good laugh.' *Well, he did, anyway, and Steff,* Hannah can't remember finding much of it funny, *though I might have done once.*

'Sold any more of his soul?' Lawrence persists.

She takes the mug and plate proffered and forces some of the hot liquid and a crust down her. It's possible it might come right back up. 'I know, I know,' she says, pressing her fingertips into her forehead. 'He used to be such a promising journalist, interested in serious news, and now he's just a celebrity hack, ya-di-da-di-da. And Steff's a—'

'Steff's a bitch.'

'You have to be to get on in their world.'

Lawrence humphs and comes to sit beside her at the large wooden table which has pride of place in his big kitchen-dining room. Even this early in the year, by mid-morning there's light coming across the little yard at the back of the house where he

24

grows some herbs and roses in pots, and through the window to bounce off the shiny, damson-coloured unit doors. It's always warm in here because of the metal Rayburn. Eyes closed, Hannah rests her head against his shoulder for a moment, inhaling his almond-wash smell. He pats her head and encourages her to eat and drink a bit more. She does so; it all goes down a little easier this time.

Lawrence continues, 'I wouldn't care so much if he didn't jerk you around.'

'We're just friends.'

'Friends don't break their promises like he has done over and over. The problem is, he's still trying to work out what his proclivities are.'

You can talk, Hannah might have said if she was feeling mean, remembering the succession of Young Turks who have left Lawrence broken-hearted but whom most of his own friends know nothing about.

'He changes his sexual preferences with his socks,' Lawrence finishes.

Hannah assures him she's fine, they were just having fun, and says she will have some more toast. He asks her about the other people on her course, obviously probing for someone who might replace Rickie. She's astonished that she initially thinks of Frederick Gough, less surprised when Clarke Stone comes to mind, but it's the irritating James Staidman she talks about. 'Not the least bit attractive,' she responds to Lawrence's enquiry. 'He obviously fancies himself, though, and thinks I do too.' The aspirin she's taken is beginning to have an effect so she starts to leaf through the newspapers Lawrence has scattered across one end of the table. There's something dull about more economic bad news and an interview with Iceland's newly elected PM, on being a woman in power and a lesbian.

'There's a piece in there about your Dr Themis Greene,' he says.

Her stomach pitches again; she holds tighter to her mug until she's steady once more. There's an obituary and she begins

25

to read through it. Dr Themis Greene, prominent psychotherapist, found battered to death. Hannah starts to skim over the details through squinted eyes. She notices Dr Greene was aged sixty-seven and thinks she looked at least ten years younger even with a caved-in skull. Then sees that her civil partnership had been preceded by a four-year relationship with another woman and a thirty-year traditional marriage. *Being a renowned therapist obviously doesn't make you less fucked up when it comes to choosing life partners,* she grins to herself. There's a list of books she's written, something about the professional organisation she led for a while, all pretty dull.

'Mike Lloyd rang,' Lawrence says when he sees she's finished reading. 'Said he'd heard you'd, you know, found Dr Greene, and he wants to interview you. He thinks there's more of a story than's being told.'

'Why?'

'Well, for a start-off, her real name's Thelma Green, without an "e".'

'Anyone can change their name, doesn't have to be suspicious.'

'Depends what you do it for. She may not even be a Doctor.'

'It's for a PhD. She's never claimed to be a medical one.' Though, of course, Lawrence would know that. Hannah is feeling distinctly prickly; she needs a shower and to get to the hairdresser. She tries standing up. 'I don't want to speak to Mike, he's abrupt and arrogant.'

Lawrence is resting back against the counter behind him. He's grown his beard back, a thin dark line outlining his square chin, and is there more grey in the hair that flops around his temples? He is smiling, bringing a blue spark to his eyes. 'Yet you spend an evening with Quirkey.' She knows he'll keep Lloyd away from her. He asks her if she has any plans; she says what they are, adding, 'And gym tomorrow. I haven't been since I left and I'm feeling distinctly unfit.'

'I thought you'd have taken to rambling the moors.'

'Oh, no.' She shivers. 'Do you want me for something?'

'Just a bit of copy-editing. You'd get paid, of course.'

'Your Baruch Spinoza book? Thought they'd got someone to fill in for me at your publishers for that.'

'She's not half as good as you.' He comes over and plants a kiss on the crown of her head. How can she refuse? Anyway she needs the money: last night had practically cleaned her out; she'd forgotten how expensive London is.

Chapter 5

Agatha Begood is concerned and Hannah feels the genuineness of it. No-one else has bothered to ask how she might be feeling back in the building where The Incident happened. Lawrence had been worried: the slight nick at the top of his long nose had shown that; but all he had said was, 'You don't have to go back, you know.' The question, 'How are you feeling?' does not come easily to Lawrence, though Hannah knows it is often behind his other enquiries or statements. Hannah has already given an evasive response to Agatha, only the other woman is not giving up that easily. She reminds Hannah of a terrier determinedly scratching a crab out of its shell — if the tall, neat Agatha could ever be said to be reminiscent of a scruffy little dog. Perhaps slightly, with her small eyes and snout, though her finely lined rice-paper skin and soft cloud of grey hair remind Hannah more of some marble statue of Minerva.

She tries to come up with a meaningful phrase for her mix of emotions. Vaguely nauseous at the thought of That Room being upstairs, even though she knows the body is gone and it is being completely cleaned and redecorated. There's anxiety which is ticking away inside her most of the time. She had begun to be more aware of it in London, when sudden moments of panic had rendered her fleetingly paralysed in crowds and on the Underground. It was why she had come back to Scarborough early. Even here, in amongst these people, most of whom she doesn't know, she isn't as confident as she might have been. She is glad Agatha has sought her out; she tells her briefly about the anxiety as it is such an oddity to her. 'Usually I'd be working this room, no problem at all.'

'It could be post-traumatic stress.'

'Isn't that what people get when they've killed someone in a war?' *What does Agatha know about me?* 'I don't think so.' Her tone is disparaging.

'Well, you've had a trauma,' says Agatha sternly.

Hannah has another glimpse of the terrier. 'Thanks for your concern, Agatha,' she says peaceably. 'I do appreciate it.'

She takes a sip of the cheap wine made worse by being served in a plastic cup. Gazing round the room she adds, 'They're a rum lot, aren't they?' The training room is full and there are more people in the corridor: colleagues, friends, former and current students, relatives, maybe a few clients, who knew? There's a PowerPoint loop running, projecting photos of Dr Themis Greene onto one wall. From this Hannah has been able to identify her ex-husband and her current wife in the crowd, her middle lover is a no-show. Hannah watches the images flip round again. She sees Themis Greene grow from a tall gangly lass with intense dark eyes in a heart-shaped face, to a tall, stately woman in fine, tailored suits, with intense dark eyes under arched eyebrows. Her life companions are stunningly alike, even the husband; they are waifs, their thin faces weighed down by lustrous black wavy hair and wide-lidded gazes, lovingly turned on Dr Greene. Though since his divorce, Dr Greene's husband has reappropriated his own surname, filled out substantially and cut his now white hair ruthlessly short. Frederick has toned down his shirt for the occasion and is talking earnestly to his fellow trainer and business partner, Orwell Winters, who is also going to be Hannah's supervisor. Always a conservative dresser, he is in a navy suit, his grey hair and beard both braided. Hannah has an even greater desire to leave and might have slunk away if Tina Russett hadn't appeared. She's puffing and sweaty and looks awkward in her black jacket and skirt. 'Am I late?'

'For what?' Agatha asks, tweezered eyebrow raised.

Oh, leave her alone, Hannah wants to say; instead she pats Tina's chubby shoulder and assures her she's missed nothing. Tina gulps down the orange juice and makes a face; Hannah presumes it's as vile as the wine. The younger woman launches into a tale about why she wasn't on time, which seems to include cooking her fiancé breakfast, popping in on her parents, who needed her to sort out some issue over their invalidity benefits, and then absolutely having to take her parents' neighbour's cat to the vet's because he'd probably been poisoned — the cat not the neighbour, Hannah ascertains — and

29

the neighbour was too upset to drive — and a taxi was for some reason beyond the pale. Tina finishes with a half-sob, tears collecting in her lovely green eyes.

Hannah puts her hand on Tina's shoulder again and gives it a squeeze. 'Oh well, you're here now, that's all that matters, eh?' She knows it is a Tina-esque statement, and the other woman immediately rallies. The three of them begin to debate the pros and cons of having had a week off training. Agatha is impatient to get on with the course. Tina has been relieved to have time to try and catch up, she is so behind. And Hannah? Hannah has been pleased to not have to come in, but has also unaccountably missed it. Their chat is brought to a halt by some ahem-ing and spoons-on-glasses clinking, Frederick is about to speak. Luckily, despite his girth he is tall, so his round, fair face, rouging now around the ears, bobs above the heads of everyone else. He welcomes all present and then says theatrically, 'I have come to praise Caesar, not to bury her.' There is a ripple of appreciation which goes through the room. Frederick waits for it before going on, saying Dr Themis Greene had been a dear and enduring friend and mentor to him, then about Dr Greene's importance to the psychotherapy world, how she had striven for a greater professionalism in terms of training and ethics (at which Hannah hears a muttering circulate the room) and how she had single-handedly given talking therapies a higher and more positive media profile. Frederick finishes, 'We will all have our own memories of Themis; mine will be of a generous and inspiring woman.' And his final 'Thank you to you all for coming,' is a croak. So it is Orwell, unseen amongst the throng, who proposes a toast. Hannah forgets and takes a good swig of her drink and then chokes, Agatha and Tina slap her on the back, making it worse, and people turn to look. Hannah's face glows scarlet, she tries laughing it off and wishes fervently that she could be elsewhere.

Her coughing attack allows James to find them. Hannah is even more intent on getting away. As he starts to interrogate them about the essay they've been given, she makes her excuses. James blocks her route; another time, then, he'd really like to get her opinion on the question, he's got so much to learn about essay writing, he's sure she could help him in that. Yes, yes, yes, one of those inexplicable spasms of panic is taking hold of her, she's not sure she can even make her legs move, but she does, she squeezes past James and is able to walk away, hoping the shaking is not visible to anyone around her. She decides she must first visit the toilets on the first floor, and finds this does steady her a little. She comes out onto the landing where an arched, stained-glass window is throwing a mosaic of reds, blues and yellows onto the carpet. Below her is the hubbub she has to get through if she is going to exit the building and just to her left is That Room, for the moment off-limits to everyone except the decorators. Voices are mounting the stairs, she realises she has no escape as she cannot make herself move in the direction of That Room. So she drags a smile up from somewhere to greet Frederick, who is accompanied by the policeman she met before but now can't name and another man who she thinks she's seen around the building a few times.

'Ah, Hannah.' Fred is disconcerted, stopped in mid-flow. There's an awkward moment.

'Is this one of your students, Fred?' asks the one who isn't the police officer. He has a soft face framed by wispy dark-brown hair to his shoulders. 'I'm Ben Cartwright, a colleague of Fred's.'

'Hannah, Hannah Poole.' She gathers herself to face the other one. 'And I'm sorry, I've forgotten your...' Then she blurts, 'Weren't your glasses red last time?' The frames match the ochre lining on his brown suit and the dye of his tie.

'DS Theo Akande, how observant, you should think of joining the force.' He is smiling, but Hannah can't tell whether he's truly relaxed with what she's said or angry or being sarcastic.

'Yes, one of my current students, and after two months' training with me she's ready to see clients.' Fred has obviously re-found his presence. 'Enjoying yourself, Hannah? Nice little gathering. What did you think of my speech?'

She hesitates. 'It went fine.' A hint of disappointment rucks his brow and she adds quickly, 'Good; yes it was good.'

'Wanted to give a decent send-off to Themis.'

'Thelma,' Hannah says automatically.

'What?'

'She was called Thelma, wasn't she?' She looks from face to face and sees agreement in only one of them.

'So we understand,' says Akande. 'How did you know?'

'A friend, a journalist friend told me.'

'She was called Thelma Greene?' Fred says with some dismay.

'Without an "e",' adds Hannah quietly. 'You didn't know?'

Fred turns to Akande and says rather more loudly than necessary that he hasn't got all day, that they should get on.

'I thought you would want to devote as much time as necessary to finding out what had happened to Dr Greene,' says Akande mildly; again Hannah detects an undercurrent of sarcasm.

'Of course, of course,' Fred says and then ushers the policeman on round the landing to his office.

Hannah is unsteady again, she grasps the heavy wooden banister and gasps like she's received a blow to her lungs.

'Are you OK?'

She hadn't realised Ben hadn't followed the others. She says she's all right and tries to straighten, only nothing in her body is cooperating.

'Take it easy.' Ben is close by her side. 'Perhaps you'd like to sit down for a bit.'

Hannah shakes her head. 'Don't you have to speak to the detective?'

'My alibi's been verified. I was coming upstairs to pick up some paperwork when I caught up with Theo.'

'You know him?'

'Small town. Wouldn't you like me to get you a drink?' He chuckles. 'You're right, it is all pretty dire.' Hannah's expression must have said it all.

She has managed to straighten. 'I'm going home.' Having established she is going to walk and in which direction she will be going, Ben offers to accompany her as his car is parked up that end of the Esplanade. Hannah thinks about refusing; however, if he's going that way anyway, it would seem odd and she is finding his closeness reassuring. 'How about the paperwork?'

'It can wait.'

The sun in the clear sky is deceptive, the chill is still damp, especially in the shadows made by the lofty brick Victorian terraces and white wedding-cake apartments which lead them down to the Esplanade. Here they are on breezy cliffs above the honey-coloured Gothic Spa across from the castle on its headland – one of Picasso's cubist faces daubed on the azure background. The sea is below them. Its solid air-force blue cracked open only occasionally by a filament of white. It has retreated away from the brown sand and weedy rocks and is quiet, with only a whisper coming in on its frosty exhale. Hannah has asked the usual questions about Ben's work — some private, some EAP work for local companies. Did he know Dr Greene? 'Only by reputation.' Then she is arrested by the brooding waves, her eyes searching out the smudged line between water and sky.

'Must be hard for you having to go back into the house after finding the body?'

'Had to do it sometime, Fred wasn't going to let me off the training hours.'

'Did you ask him?'

'Didn't see the point, I was sure he wouldn't understand.'

'He might have done. He's more pliant than he can appear.'

'Is he?'

'In my experience.'

They begin walking up the Esplanade. Hannah notices little spears of green nudging up above the brown earth under the bare-armed trees. She wants to know what he knows about The Incident, what's generally known, and he complies unhesitatingly.

'From what Fred said there was no forced entry, so whoever it was had a key or was let in. And from the questions the police were asking, I don't think they believe it was a random attack.'

'So it was most probably someone she knew? But they don't know who yet?' The tremor which had started in Hannah's spine is in danger of developing into more general shaking as if she's caught a fever. She becomes absorbed in appearing less perturbed than she is. Ben seems to think she is worried about her own safety and gives a reassurance (a rather spurious one in Hannah's opinion) that Dr Greene's killer would be unlikely to be interested in hurting anyone else. Hannah wishes fervently that he would shut up and go away. She is relieved when he stops by a car, a sporty red number, and says that it is his. She says her goodbyes quickly and starts to walk on.

'Will you be OK?'

She turns. 'Of course.'

'Here.' He's holding out a card. 'If you ever want to talk.'

She takes it just to get rid of him.

Chapter 6

'Why are you here, Hannah?' asks Frederick Gough.

Fuck off, Hannah wants to say. Instead she firmly presses her lips together and takes on what she hopes will be interpreted as a reflective air. How she hates these two hours of 'processing' at the beginning of each training day. At first they had startled her, the concept that anyone in their group of five could just say anything, whatever was in their heads, and take the consequences; it was way beyond her comprehension. She had tried to throw in the odd comment, carefully thought-through before offered, but no-one had really taken much notice. It was as if she was invisible. Her colleagues were more practised, more used to each other, since she had joined them in their third and final year. After a while she had begun to dread the two hours, becoming increasingly convinced that whatever she said would be wrong, so she had kept her mouth closed for the most part, though she then feared she would indeed disappear. Now she hates every second of it. What a stupid idea: human civilization wouldn't last a minute if everyone behaved like this. There was nothing to be learned from people emptying their undigested thoughts onto the carpet.

'What is it that you're trying not to say, Hannah?' asks Gough His tall round figure is relaxed back into the armchair, his stubby fingers clasped over the dome of his stomach, clad today in a swirl of blue and lemon silk. He does not appear that concerned whether she responds or not. However, Hannah knows she is being watched very carefully.

Fuck off, she doesn't say again. Slowly she gives the impression of rousing herself from her contemplation. 'I'm here for the same thing everyone else is here for, Fred.'

'Don't talk for me, Hannah,' snaps Clarke Stone, his lean, black-jeaned leg jiggling. There's a ripple of agreement amongst the others.

Hannah grins and apologises. *Oh, just fuck right off,* she thinks. *All of you.*

Agatha, immaculately turned out as usual, her gossamer-grey hair is twisted up into an intricate, plaited whorl, says that she's here to learn more about herself. James and Tina agree from either end of the sofa which takes up the wall under the window. James Staidman then moves his rectangular bulk forward and begins to talk ponderously about never having had the freedom before to truly be himself, how he had gone too early into marriage, into fatherhood, had become lost in trying to meet the needs and expectations of his family. The others in the group listen intently, even though they have heard it all before. *And here comes the stuff about his mother,* thinks Hannah. *Wait for it, wait for it, and, yes, his mother telling him she'd have preferred another girl because she had enough sons.* James becomes tearful and Tina makes sympathetic noises. *What are you doing?* Hannah carefully keeps her distaste from her face. *We've heard it all a million times.If he's serious about learning more about himself, he could start by realising how effing boring he is.* Tina begins to talk quietly about being the daughter of deaf parents and sister to a brother with cerebral palsy, about always being the caring one, having to look out for others. Hannah feels sad, she wants to say this, maybe go over and hold the hunched, plump Tina. As usual she's too slow, Agatha has found the right thing to say and James has held Tina's hand for a moment before she delicately withdraws it to clasp the other one in her lap. Clarke's jiggling has taken over the whole of his short, taut, muscle-defined body, 'You're all talking rot. If you were being honest you'd say you were doing this to further your career or cos you want forty quid an hour.'

'I thought we weren't going to talk for each other,' says Agatha sternly.

'OK, I'll speak for myself, shall I?' Clarke continues to talk rapidly about how he doesn't need to know more about himself, he already has a very clear understanding, thank you very much and, like all humans, his main impulse is to make money, he wants a comfortable life, one where he won't have to worry about paying the bills, where he can take a holiday without being

36

concerned. Hannah remembers his stories of his family's accumulating debts when his dad was made redundant. 'You're not going to tell me,' Clarke says crossly, 'any of you are doing this for self-improvement or for some altruistic "I want to help people" motivation.' Here Tina appears to wake up and mutters her disagreement. Clarke ignores her and finishes, 'Humans are about self-interest, pure and simple.'

'Don't talk for me, Clarke,' Agatha repeats more quietly, as if she's had a pummelling.

After a short pause, Frederick Gough rouses himself. 'Well, we've a few minutes left. And,' his gaze swivels towards Hannah, 'I still haven't had an answer to my question, Hannah: what are you doing here?'

Hannah finds herself unaccountably close to tears: *he hasn't forgotten me.* It's Lawrence's comment which comes to mind: 'You never finish anything, this'll go the way of your accountancy training and the plumbing course. You've tried to get this counselling qualification twice before and you've not got through to the end, I don't imagine this time will be any different.' Cautiously, as if feeling her way into a new language, Hannah says, 'I am going to finish something, Frederick; for once in my life, I am going to complete something I've started.'

He smiles. 'Well done, Hannah.'

She feels bathed in a sunlamp until Clarke butts in: 'Well that must be the first honest thing I've heard you say.'

She smiles and nods. *And you can fuck right off, you supercilious little toad.*

'Right,' says Frederick Gough, rubbing a stubby hand over his bald head. 'Let's take a break.' And he leaves rapidly, followed by Clarke, Agatha and James. Hannah is about to go with them, then she stops noting, Tina's stillness. She goes over and sits close, sliding her arm across Tina's polyester-clad back. For a brief moment the young woman relaxes into this half, rather tense, hug, then she gets up swiftly. 'Coffee Hannah? Think Agatha's brought in some of her lemon drizzle.'

'Oh goody,' Hannah says with forced relish: she would have preferred to stay sitting quietly with Tina. It is not to be, so she jumps up with as much vigour as she can muster. 'Let's go, then.'

Chapter 7

The whole enterprise has been such a mistake. Why Aurora
thought she could just nip to the supermarket any ore is now
beyond her. She had struggled to shower and get dressed in
something that made her feel half-human. She had struggled to
drive and to park. She had struggled with the trolley and halfway
round she had wanted to lie down in the aisle to sleep. She had
given up on most of her shopping list; even so she had struggled
to get the bags into the car. And currently she is struggling to get
them back out again. *What an idiot girl,* she is telling herself.
*Why, why, why couldn't I have left it until Max got back from
football? You're just too headstrong for your own good, Aurora.*
Her mother used to say that. She could talk. She's the most
headstrong person in the whole world. Must be where Aurora
gets it from. She can't lean over to get any proper purchase on
the last bag, so she grabs at it and pulls; somehow as it exits the
boot it gets snagged and slips from her grasp so that its contents
of packets of frozen peas and salmon, along with pots of
yoghurts, end up spilling onto the driveway. The noise that
comes from her mouth is a cross between a hyena being
strangled and a hungry guinea pig. The awfulness of the sound
produces sobs and tears. *Fool girl, you're a fool girl,* Aurora
repeats silently.

'Are you OK?' asks a woman's voice.

Aurora doesn't look round, instead she hastily tries to
gain some control, saying she's fine and no, she doesn't need any
help, her voice quavering. Once she thinks the person has moved
on, and with one hand on the car steadying her, she attempts to
pick up her groceries.

'Here, let me do that.' Un-swollen hands on the ends of
nimble arms quickly gather the packets and pots back into the
bag, then a body stands up from crouching in one easy
movement. Aurora remembers when she could do that, as she
slowly unbends. She's looking at a woman of about her own age,
sturdy, some inches shorter but then, most women are. Her hair
looks ironed with some burgundy highlights. She has careful

make-up around deep-hazel eyes and is dressed in smart black jeans and a tailored navy wool jacket.

'Hannah,' the woman says stiffly. 'From next door. I was passing and heard you crying out and mumbling to yourself.'

Aurora feels the heat in her cheeks intensify. She tries to explain about the bag and the shopping.

'Well, I'm glad it's only that,' Hannah says, looking relieved. 'I thought maybe you'd gone into labour.' She urges Aurora to go indoors and put the kettle on, she'll sort out the shopping.

Aurora is pleased the kitchen has remained relatively tidy since Rose blitzed it and she prepares a brew for them both while directing Hannah on where things need to be stored. Then she sits with an unappealing grunt and indicates a chair for her guest to take. She recalls that Max said old Stan and Val Poole were having their daughter to stay for some kind of training course, so she asks Hannah about it. When Hannah finishes her responses, Aurora comments, 'A year doesn't sound long enough to train to be a counsellor.'

'It's intensive and I've done some courses previously. It'll be three years all told, and then I have to do my client hours and write a case study before I get accredited.'

'Sounds a bit like what I did for my solicitor's qualification, mix of theory and practice.' *And doesn't that feel like a long time ago, a world away, when I still had energy and drive.* Hannah asks the usual questions about how long Aurora has before she gives birth and shakes her head rather too fervently when asked if she has children. Aurora makes an effort not to feel resentful. She asks about Dr Greene and how the Centre has been affected, only Hannah appears reluctant to say much, so the conversation moves on to the frustrations Hannah feels about living in a small town when she's used to having London on her doorstep. It's easy chat, and Aurora can feel herself getting more dozy. The kitchen is warm and the very faint suggestion of sun outside is being amplified by the French windows at her back. The banging of the front door and Max calling her name filters through the haze and then the room is full with noise and boisterous men: Max has brought someone home with him. Ben, normally fairly diffident, has been infected by his friend, or maybe it's the football that has got his testosterone up. Anyway, they are both talking loudly and rapidly and laughing at things Aurora does not find funny. She looks over at Hannah, who is smiling in a polite, restrained way. Aurora raises her eyes heavenward, and Hannah mouths the word, 'boys', and they both chuckle.

Apparently, there is a plan afoot for Max to join Ben in a jaunt to a pub to hear a local band. Aurora's good humour drains completely away. She fixes her husband with a glare. *How could he even think that was a good idea? After he'd been out enjoying himself all morning. And I've had to get the shopping done. And I'm so tired. Doesn't he get how tired I am?* 'I thought you'd agreed you'd help me with some chores this afternoon,' she says forcefully.

'I can do those tomorrow.'

'No, I want them done today!' Her exclamation is followed by an abrupt hush. Everyone in the room is tensed and looking at her.

Max begins to speak, 'Now hang on Aurora ...' But Ben interrupts, telling him it's OK, they can go another time. 'Best stay with Aurora, mate,' he finishes very quietly. Max's jaw is jutting out, Aurora can see he is in a mood to argue, only Ben's hand on his sleeve makes him hesitate. There is another pause. Then Hannah says she ought to be going and Ben takes the opportunity to escape too. Aurora automatically urges them to come again soon as they leave, then feels deflated. 'Lunch?' she offers feebly.

'I need to clean my kit first,' says Max. She knows he will take himself off with his sulk for over an hour. She is enormously hungry and yet too exhausted to move.

****

Boredom can get you into all sorts of messes. Hannah sits on a bench seat in the corner of a pub she would normally have avoided. She watches a group of folksy-looking players setting up, while Ben fetches drinks; yes, boredom has a lot to answer for.

In truth it had been more than boredom that had propelled her out of the house earlier in the day. Her mother was out doing her turn in the WRVS café at the hospital, and her father was grating on her. She had spent a restless night and had finally slept from about 7am, so had not emerged for breakfast until ten. This brought a lecture from her father about lazing around and wasting her life, before she had even made herself coffee. She tried to defend herself, pointing out that in a few years she would be a qualified counsellor, and he said he doubted it and anyway, what kind of career was that? He was bristling, his face sharp as leaded type. So she said he was probably right and sat down with her mug to survey the papers. There was more about the 'most serious global economic turmoil in sixty years' and some president wanted for crimes against humanity. *Great.* Hannah turned the pages until she found the crossword. She had expected her father to go up to his office, but he was still stomping about. It was then she had looked up and seen how diminished he was, his thinning hair revealing patches of flaky scalp. She wanted to say something, ask him how he was, only one glance at his stiff mouth told her to hold her peace. She finished her drink quickly. She felt the force of him shoving her out, not only from the kitchen, but also from the house.

She took the winding overgrown path down the cliff to the beach, grateful for some milder air. There were birds chirruping, not that she could identify any of them. A blackbird — even she knows that one — landed close to her, picking up a twig in his startlingly yellow beak from a tangle of bramble and gorse, before flying off again. As she approached the beach she could smell the sharp tang of seaweed and briny water caught in amongst the rocks fringing the sand. The sea was calm, dense, lapping delicately at the land, a cat rhythmically cleaning its fur.

She had sat on the concrete storm wall watching the water for some time. She was arguing with her dad, telling him that this time she would finish, she would become, become something, something he could be proud of. Sadness came with that thought: she wouldn't ever manage that. Even her brother, Stephen, had problems in that quarter, despite being a successful financial consultant. He'd apparently managed to remain unaffected by the present economic calamities. 'Stay one step ahead of the game, Hannah, that's all it takes,' he had said to her the other evening on the phone. She hadn't a clue what he was talking about and hadn't bothered to ask. Stephen, however, had their mother's undying devotion. *Not that he's grateful for it*.

They would all be going over tomorrow to Stephen's swanky house in York for Sunday lunch with him, his wife and their two sons. It would be sheer agony. Veronica, her sister-in-law, would have made an enormous spread, which she would pick at and Stephen would wolf down. She would regale them with the ills of all the neighbours and probe her in-laws for any tragedies she could exploit. Hannah's mother would eat and drink too much and stare adoringly at Stephen, asking him endless inane questions. Stan Poole, the once renowned and steely newspaper editor, would shake with his own impotence at not being able to bring the whole farce to a swift and brutal conclusion.

Hannah had never enjoyed family get-togethers, had avoided them when she could, and her move to London had given her plenty of excuses; now, however, she saw the scenario with greater clarity than she ever had before. She saw how each person played their part in creating the torturous scene. Even she did. Smiling and passive, accepting Veronica's confidences about how worried she is that Val might be going senile. 'Early onset, Hannah, I know about these things,' Veronica would say, making allusion to her nurse training some twenty years previously, though she had barely practised before becoming a full-time mother. And Hannah always squashed the response she would have liked to give: 'You know what, Veronica, just mind your own fucking business.' Preferring instead to let it slide, let everything slide.

Feeling annoyed, Hannah had jumped up and walked at a fast pace along the beach a short way, then up the path by the Spa through the grey beech-tree trunks to the Esplanade, turning back towards her parents' house. As she began to approach, she slowed; she did not want to return just yet, though she didn't want to be alone with her own thoughts either. So it was that she was sauntering past her parents' neighbours when she heard an alarming screech and a woman talking to herself, and peeping into the drive she saw a heavily pregnant woman looking like she might be in the throes of childbirth. Hannah's first instinct had been to move off quickly, then she took the decision that had landed her in this pub. That decision and boredom.

Ben returns with a couple of plates of palatable-looking sandwiches, a red wine for her and a pint of brown beer for him.

'Thanks,' she says. 'And thanks for the reprieve, I couldn't have faced the long, tedious afternoon with my parents.' She wants him to know she wasn't coming on to him when she suggested she accompany him instead of Max. However, she then realises how this might sound and tries to retrieve the situation by saying it's about time she got into the life of Scarborough a bit more. He says he supposes she must find it very dull after London in a way that suggests to Hannah that he too is regretting ending up in this situation. After an awkward pause for some munching and sipping, she asks him some questions about himself — always, she has found, a safe option, especially with men. Ben appears less eager than some to talk about himself; even so she discovers that he grew up in a village near Scarborough and yes, he did spend several years in London, which he enjoyed, when he was younger. He'd been quite peripatetic during a period travelling through Thailand, Malaysia, Australia, working when he could, mainly manual or bar jobs; but he is now content to be settled back in Yorkshire. His dad and brother (now married with children) still live in the village working for British Gas as engineers. His mother died when he was a baby. Hannah is startled by this imparted piece of tragedy and mutters some inadequate platitude. Halfway through the sandwiches he begins to tease things out of her, how she likes the anonymity of London, though this last time she had started to feel uneasy in the crowds. *Why do I admit this to him?* She isn't a native of Scarborough, her parents moved here after she'd left home, for her father's job. They were always moving for that, she'd been to six schools by the time she was sixteen, all in different corners of the UK.

'That can't have been easy,' he says.

'Oh, you know.' She's finished her wine and is contemplating another one. 'Toughens you up. How about you? Were you schooled around here?'

'Thornby Manor, a grammar school in York.'

'Sounds posh.' There's something familiar about the name, only she can't nail it down immediately.

'Scholarship boy,' Ben says rapidly.

She suggests another round and he accepts readily. The musicians have finally tuned up and got themselves together by the time she returns and she and Ben sit companionably listening to the first set. Hannah finds herself enjoying it, they are surprisingly accomplished; drums, acoustic guitarist who also sings with deep bluesy tones, electric base and a soaring sax. Hannah wishes she had stuck at some music lessons; but then, they hadn't been anywhere long enough for her to get into anything at all and after she realised the decampments were going to be regular she gave up trying. Like she gave up trying to make friends in any meaningful way or make any particular effort in class. What did it matter if she flopped, she'd be starting somewhere new in a short while anyway. Most of the time she passed under the radar, irrevocably average, the majority of her teachers not noticing when she was there nor when she was gone. The singer moodily croons out the last number: 'You've got a friend.' Hannah begins to feel tearful. When the music comes to an end, Ben gently touches her elbow, 'You OK?'

She smiles swiftly, nodding, 'Comes of drinking wine in the middle of the day.' Then she remembers, 'Lawrence.'

'I'm sorry?'

'Lawrence went to Thornby Manor too. I don't suppose you know him, though I guess you're about the same age. Lawrence Fielding?' She begins to fill in some detail, fatherless Lawrence brought up by mother and aunts in Colchester and sent to Thornby Manor as a boarder on some legacy left by his dad. (Though he's recently discovered his father was departed not deceased.) Currently journalist, writer and radio broadcaster.

Ben is nodding his head. 'Yes I knew Lawrence, a couple of years above me at school. That must have been a shock for him about his dad. I remember that was what brought us together in some ways, losing a parent when young. He kind of took me under his wing, misfits united, we were quite close at one time.'

'Really?'

He chuckles. 'I've always been boringly heterosexual; being a scholarship boy marked me out. I didn't join Lawrence in his adolescent experimentation. Though I did give him his first joint, I believe. We lost touch when I went travelling and he got caught up in being a newshound.'

'You didn't fall out, then?' She knows Lawrence closed the door on his schooldays very firmly.

'Oh no, Lawrence was pretty committed to his career and I didn't have one; was, well, dropping out. And, of course, keeping in touch then was harder.' He smiles. 'No text, email, Facebook, you know.'

'Prehistoric,' she laughs.

'Exactly,' he says, joining her.

She notices the cinnamon in his eyes, the way his nutmeg hair curls a little around his ears. She's never been one for long hair on men, but it matches his slightly pallid Byronic cast. He's average height, compact. He's wearing black. He was wearing a black suit and dark shirt last time; this time it's black jeans, black roll-neck and black hiking jacket, the sort you might go up

46

Helvellyn in, or so Hannah supposes. The only hint of colour comes in the thin stripe of green in his scarf. She can see him coming to his decision, even the weighing-up of the pros and cons, before he asks her if she would like him to show her a bit of the town. 'Unless,' he adds quickly, 'you have other plans?' She senses that maybe he wouldn't be overly sorry if she did have somewhere else to go and considers refusing his offer. She checks her watch, three-ten. The alternatives are an afternoon on her own, or she does have an essay to finish. Neither appeals. So she says yes.

Outside the fuggy atmosphere of the pub, the day is bright and sharp, pale-blue sky appears between grey cloud scraped thin. Ben walks fast and Hannah has to put some effort into keeping up with him. He talks about what got him to train as a psychotherapist: the Australian girlfriend who left him, saying he needed therapy, and his subsequent first brush with counselling in Adelaide. This got him interested enough to do a beginner's psychology course before returning to the UK to train properly, about thirteen years previously, when he was twenty-five. 'How about you? What brought you into training?'

'I'm not sure, really.' She is scurrying, and wondering about suggesting they take a bus. 'I've tried different things. I work as a copy-editor and proofreader for Lawrence's publishers. He got me the job and I enjoy it, only, I don't know.' She pauses to pant, 'It's not something Lawrence understands about.'

'And that's important?'

'I suppose so, yes. I mean, I could easily go on rooming with him, working for him, relying on him, but, you know, I'm going to be thirty-three this year, I should be ... I need to... I need to get on with something,' she finishes, running out of words and air. She has not articulated this before.

'Coming out from under Lawrence's wing?'

'I suppose so, yes. Maybe grow up a little?' She's surprising herself with her candour. 'About time, eh?' She forces a laugh. This time he doesn't join in with her. They reach the park, take its steep path leading to the lake where an artificial island stands tall in the middle, topped by a pagoda resplendent in red and gold. Hannah sits down on the first bench they come to, puts her hands in her jacket pockets: it's colder than the sun gleaming off the water and the gold paint would suggest.

He sits beside her. 'You OK?'

'The walk, it was a bit further than I expected.'

'Oh.' He looks disappointed.

'It ... it was worth it, though.' She gazes around appreciatively.

'I love it,' he says with some force.

'I've got a bit out of shape, that's all. I haven't joined a gym here.'

'I don't like gyms, no need when you can walk and cycle in such gorgeous countryside.'

They sit for a while watching the Canada geese and mallard ducks squabbling over territory. Hannah thinks maybe it's time to say goodbye and get a taxi home. However, the warmth from the sun begins to filter through and she catches glimpses of green buds pushing out from the twig fingers of the trees. *It is lovely.* She relaxes into the moment, closes her eyes. After a few minutes he suggests going to a café before they begin their walk home; perhaps he has taken pity on her. Conversation flows again, they discover a shared liking for the Conchords and a shared delight in France, even that they both have a spattering of French, Hannah having spent nine months doing bar work in Nice. 'I came back when I ran out of money,' she says, feeling the shame once more. 'To be rescued by Lawrence again.'

'He's the rescuing type.'

'Is he?'

'Enjoys having one or two lame lambs in tow.'

'And I'm a lame lamb,' she says. He pinkens a little and is about to protest. She cuts him off. 'No, you're right. It's about time I stood on my own four hoofs.' She smiles and he follows suit; he has a pleasant, gentle smile. 'So, Benjamin.' She looks out of the café window and sees the sea is more turbulent, mirroring the grey now clotting the sky. 'Ready for the trek back, looks brisk.'

'We can get the bus if you like.'

'No, no, it'll do me good.' She puts on her leather gloves, knowing they will be ineffectual.

'Here.' He hands her a knitted hat. 'I've a spare one.'

She hesitates and then pulls it on, thinking, *This is Scarborough, who's going to see? Who's going to care?*

'And it's Benedick,' he says as they begin to walk.

'Sorry?'

'Benedick, not Benjamin.'

'Ah, a "Much Ado" fan?'

'My mum was.'

It takes a few steps for Hannah to find the right words. 'It must have been hard for you, her dying when you were small?'

And he takes a few steps to respond, then he says that what was hard was having no-one to tell him about her as his dad and brother wouldn't speak about her, or her death. 'It was a very male household: lots of footy, beer, fish and chips on a Saturday night. I missed ... I didn't know what I was missing, only that it wasn't there.'

'The female influence.'

He nods.

'That's where Lawrence came in?'

He chuckles. 'And luckily there were women in the street who kind of adopted me. Rose Short in particular; she moved in next door when I was about eleven, she'd known Mum from way back, then gone off to London and abroad, and returned when she inherited her aunt's house. She was able to tell me about Mum when they used to hang out with each other as teenagers. So that was something. And Rose is a great cook, homemaker; well, she made herself into one, once Maya was born. It was like having a foster-mum and stepsister as neighbours.' Hannah hears the affectionate tenor in Ben's voice; she is drawn to it and then as quickly wants to say something spiteful and comments on the absent father and is told that he was a French doctor Rose met while working for Médecins Sans Frontières. 'He was and is married, but is around for Maya.'

'You still see them, then, Rose and Maya?'

He nods. 'Rose still lives next door to my dad. And my brother lives round the corner. She keeps an eye on them both, bless her. Maya, well, she's about sometimes.'

Hannah feels even less like talking about them. They're coming to the corner in Marine Drive where North Bay turns into South Bay and the gathering breeze is keener here. A fishing boat with its red-painted cabin pitches precariously as it rounds the end of the harbour wall. 'Has Theo said anything more about the Dr Greene investigation?'

Ben shakes his head. 'He wouldn't tell me what's going on, it's all confidential.'

She is disappointed. Most of the time now she manages to usher thoughts of 'The Incident' to the back of her mind, yet it lingers, with a treacherous sense of panic which peaks too often for her liking. She thinks if only they could arrest someone, the terror would disappear for her too. *Why haven't they got anywhere? Why doesn't Ben know?* 'Who do they think it was?' she asks crossly.

'Why do you think I would know?' He seems a little taken back.

She tries to moderate her voice. 'I thought you knew her, a bit.'

'She was far too high-flying to be bothered by someone like me. I get the impression she was always on the move, setting things up, moving on, tearing things down again too, so I hear. Came back to Scarborough a few days a month, other than that was off globetrotting or in her expensive villa on Jersey, or so Orwell says. I'm not sure how many real friends she had. Lots of acolytes and colleagues.'

'And she set up the Centre?'

'Yes, about fifteen years ago and she had Fred and Orwell teaching for her. There was a lot of money swilling about, by all accounts. Then Dr Greene left, what, ten, eleven years ago. Fred and Orwell bought her out. Apparently Dr Greene was very eager to release her funds quite suddenly.'

'Where was she in her complex private life? I thought therapists are supposed to be sorted themselves;, sounds like she had a problem.'

'Our intention is to be marginally more sorted than our clients,' Ben says easily. 'You sound upset.'

Hannah stops walking and leans against the concrete sea wall. Gulls screech overhead, swooping down from the castle cliff, which is hugged by the road they are on. She's beginning to feel seriously tired and cold. 'Dead bodies tend to have that effect on me.'

'Of course.' Ben gives a placating smile which annoys her even more.

'No, you don't understand, I can't get the bloody visuals out of my head, and that smell, like someone had pissed themselves, it was horrible. I don't sleep properly any more, and then there's the bloody panic attacks. You weren't there, so don't say you understand.' She turns her back, the wind spits salt into her face. *It's only a story, tell it to yourself again, only change the ending, no life-size collapse-over doll.*

'I didn't say I understood. You're right, I wasn't there, but you can tell me about it, I'm listening.'

'I've got my ruddy therapist for that,' she says into the wind.

'What?'

'Nothing.'

After a moment's consideration, he asks whether the dreams and panic attacks are new to her. She's not going to tell him she's had them before, periodically, resurfacing when she's felt under stress. She's not going to tell him anything more. 'Shall we go? It's too cold to be chatting and I want to get home.'

He acquiesces, saying something about it being the vernal equinox so the days should be getting longer and warmer. The pavement is busier here, with crowds bustling around the amusements and the shops on the foreshore; conversation is harder and Hannah doesn't feel like making any effort. At a cobbled lane heading away from the sea and jammed between a chippie and a cheap bookstore, Ben stops. 'I'm up there. It's been ...' He pauses a moment too long before supplying the word 'fun'.

'We must do it again sometime,' she replies, then regrets her sarcasm. She would like to see him another time, maybe.

'You've got my number, give me a call.' He looks like he might kiss her on her cheek, so she quickly takes a step back. She says she will and then turns to go. At the next corner, a few metres on, she looks over her shoulder. He's still standing there, watching her. She waves and he waves back. The next time she glances round, he has gone.

Chapter 8

Theo is feeling frustrated. At just after 9am, he is on his second large coffee of the day and he has retreated to one of the interview rooms to drink it. It is a mustard-painted box with a small window high up in the wall opposite the thick door and it smells faintly of cigarettes, but at least he can be alone here. DI Hoyle is pushing for him to make an arrest: he wants the case closed and they have a good enough suspect, the hapless Douglas Olds. Dr Greene's client, the last person to see Dr Greene alive and someone who can't get his story straight. What time did he leave Dr Greene? Where exactly did he go? Why did he launder all his clothing when he got home and before his wife returned from her mother's? Douglas Olds comes up with different answers each time, all of them vague. And yet Theo hesitates. 'You're not in Birmingham or Manchester now,' Hoyle says, 'This is Scarborough. If it looks and smells like the bacon factory it usually is. Olds's your man.' The DI interweaves the fingers of his ham hands.

Theo has in front of him the folder containing the various reports made and interviews taken. He flicks through it again. Forensics have not been much of a help. The murder weapon was a 'heavy implement with a circular metal protuberance of about 15 cm in circumference and 3 cm in diameter'. A hammer, then, a common-or-garden one, not been found, probably at the bottom of the sea by now if the killer had any sense. Fred Gough had thought there might have been a hammer missing from the Centre's toolbox, only he couldn't be certain and he gave the impression that it wasn't really his function to know these things, they have a handyman for all those types of jobs. The toolbox is never used, had probably been there since before Dr Greene owned the building. So the murder weapon could have been grabbed at the last minute, which would mean the killer would have to know about the toolbox in the cupboard under the stairs, or the hammer was brought in from elsewhere.

The crime scene had yielded a vast array of fingerprints and DNA traces. Hoyle had vetoed any in-depth investigation of them: it was too costly and any self-respecting defence lawyer would make short work of any results since all the main players, not to mention many, many bit-parters, were happy to admit to having been in the room during the preceding couple of weeks. The urine, Theo's one hope, turned out to be Dr Greene's own. Theo suspected it was the person who had been careful not to leave any trace that they actually wanted to speak to.

Love, money, addiction or hate, the four great motivators for the majority of crime. I can rule out addiction. Can't I? With three acknowledged relationships and, it was emerging, a number of affairs (with people of both genders) over her lifetime, love and hate have to be front-runners. Ex-husband had been at a meeting in London, current wife, Penny, had been at some poetry reading and abandoned lover, Eve, was determined not to be found. *Money, then?* The strange intricacies of Dr Greene's financial dealings are beyond Theo, yet his DI had said no funding for further digging. 'Douglas; he's your man,' he'd repeated with a smile.

And it isn't as if Theo isn't keen to get on with closing his first big case in his new job, prove himself, stop some of the rumours as to what was behind his hasty promotion. He knows what they say behind his back: fast-tracked university boy, still wet behind those black ears of his. Even so he doesn't want to take Olds in yet, *it doesn't feel right.* He imagines Hoyle laughing at this: what did feelings have to do with it? Theo drinks down the dregs from his mug. *I have to come up with something better than that.*

He takes DC Harry Shilling with him to interview Orwell Winters, having got some background from Suze before he'd left. Surprisingly, Orwell Winters is his given name; Theo was beginning to wonder whether all psychotherapists changed their names for effect. And he comes from a local family, one which used to own the big department store in town before it was taken over and changed into a Debenhams. The Winters' Haberdashery of Orwell's great-great-grandfather's time had grown and grown until it had come down to Orwell's father and his three brothers. Then it had fallen apart because the four of them couldn't agree, on anything. So Orwell had been brought up in comparative (if genteel) penury and amongst relatives riven by jealousy, blame and disappointment. His mother appears to have been the saving factor, heaping affection on her only child and boosting his confidence. One of Suze's brothers had been mates with him for a short while, though it hadn't lasted, pints on a Saturday night and a shared enjoyment in James Bond not being able to bridge the gap between Old Town and the posher suburb of Scalby. 'Nice bloke,' Suze had said, which is praise indeed. 'Or used to be.' Adding an explanation when prompted, 'Anything can happen in thirty-odd years, can't it?'

Theo is to see Orwell at his home, still in Scalby, a rambling bungalow in a large garden, with a self-contained flat on the side for the indomitable Ma Winters, going strong at the age of ninety. Orwell has his own kids, two daughters in their twenties, tall, smiling and vivacious according to the many photos cluttering the messy living room. Papers and files are everywhere. 'Comes from my wife working from home,' Orwell says, moving a folder off the sagging settee so that Theo and Harry can sit. The dark and diminutive Mrs Winters is grafting away in another room. There's a comfy atmosphere to the house. It reminds Theo of his parent's home back in Mosley, Birmingham, always filled with chatter and activity, partly from him and his three elder sisters, partly from visiting aunts, uncles and cousins. A dwelling where dark corners and solitude were hard to find.

The portly Orwell is dressed casually in jogging pants and sweatshirt; the skin on his angular face has slumped into folds, giving him the appearance of a dejected cartoon dog. Even his wispy hair and beard are shaggy. He looks tired. Theo has seen him looking better. They run through again what Winters was doing that Sunday. Most of the day had been spent en famille, with his girls, wife and mother joined by some cousins of his for lunch. In the afternoon he had met Gough at the Centre to plan a training event and go through some business questions. They had both left, having met Dr Greene on her arrival. Gough had driven off to his home in a cottage on the edge of Sheffield; though, as he lives alone, there is no definitive proof of when he arrived (and Gough appeared insulted when asked to supply it). Winters had gone for a long walk, arriving home perhaps an hour later. He needed time to clear his head, he'd said. Theo isn't happy that Gough and Winters are each other's alibi; however, their stories are consistent. And Winters was able to provide what he had been wearing (verified by a cousin) unwashed for analysis, while Gough did pop to his local for a pint at nine-thirty that night.

When Theo asks Orwell how he got on with Dr Greene, there is a hesitation. Gough had been eager to talk about his relationship with the great woman, saying it was close, uncomplicated, he was grateful for the chances Dr Greene had given him, had thought her a talented trainer and therapist. Winters pauses and Theo wonders again about the hour-long walk: could it have been longer? The afternoon gathering at his house had been chaotic enough for him to not have been missed for, say, another half an hour. Long enough for Orwell to go back after Olds had left in order to dispatch Dr Greene. Winters sighs. 'I've known Themis longer than Fred has. Thelma, as she was then, and we did some of our training together. It's no secret that we did not always see eye to eye.'

'You argued?'

Orwell nods slowly.

'About what?'

'Pretty much everything. She was something of a steamroller even then, if she saw what she wanted she'd go for it and didn't appear to care if someone got trodden on.' He looks even more unhappy.

'Did you get trodden on?' asks Harry breathily. Theo looks at her. He considers reining her back, but it is a good question.

'Once or twice, until I learnt to keep out of the way. One time she urged me to stand for this committee, I didn't want to, but she kept going on about it, so I did. Then she swoops in as a last-minute candidate and grabs the position from me. I think,' he adds quietly, 'she only did it because she could, to humiliate me.'

'So why did you accept the teaching post?'

Orwell grins. 'I needed the money. My wife, my mother, my girls.' He waves his hand like it's a fan. 'And there was a lot of money, more than at other training centres. I don't know where she got it from.'

'Did you ever find out?'

He shakes his head. 'I suspected. Thelma,' he appears to enjoy saying that name and repeats it, 'Thelma knew Russians and Ukrainians with offshore accounts before any of us realised there were Eastern Europeans with money. And her ethics: well, they weren't what you might call robust. It's not actually ethical to start living with an ex-client, you know? Anyone else would have lost their registration.'

'Only Dr Greene didn't?' Theo is distracted by a tensioning in Harry. There's been much banter about the victim's move from male to female partner. Theo had waded in when it had got too distasteful, a DC boasting he had what it takes to stop any woman straying 'to the other team', with lewd hand gestures as accompaniment. 'This is a dead person you're talking about,' Theo had shouted. *Probably didn't make myself any friends.* He'd noticed Shilling motionless on the margins.

'As I said,' Winters is answering, 'she had friends in all the right places and she collected information, if you know what I mean.'

'She blackmailed people?'

Orwell shrugged.

'What about you?' asks Harry. 'Did she have any information on you?' Theo's pleased to see her curiosity.

Again a pause. 'It's hard to be a therapist for thirty-five years without making some mistakes, but she had nothing she could sink me with, or she'd have used it.'

'Yet you stuck with her and she let you take over the business?' asksTheo, wondering if he should probe the mistakes more.

'As I said, I needed the money, and it was good to be one of Thelma's golden boys for a while. And then she needed money quick, she needed out fast.'

'Why?'

Another shrug. 'I always thought it was because her Russian friends had found that they were missing something, like a fair amount of cash.'

'You stayed friends, though?' Harry comes in.

'We were never friends,' Orwell says, almost rousing himself to some heat in his voice. 'We remained colleagues and, as long as I wasn't in her way, we were on cordial terms.'

Theo focuses on Orwell's face, sees its creases and also a pair of pine-needle-coloured eyes. He gathers himself and then says assertively, 'Did you kill Dr Greene?'

Winters scans Theo, smiles and laughs, his head back, his mane shaking. 'No. I have to get my wife to remove spiders from the bath. I haven't eaten meat since I was eighteen. I couldn't knock another human on the head until they were dead, however much I hated them.'

'Did you hate Dr Greene?' asks Harry, her pen poised.

'Maybe,' Orwell mutters, the smile draining away. 'Part of me, maybe hated her.'

'Hate can make a killer,' says Theo.

'I know, Detective Sergeant, I know.' He's looking sad again. 'I've done my years in forensic psychology. However,' he looks from Theo to Harry and back, 'I did not kill Thelma Green, without an "e". I wouldn't risk all this for having her out of my life.' His gaze travels the room, lingering on the photos.

Theo senses there is something not being said. Slowly he goes on: 'Unless Dr Greene had a piece of information that was a threat to all this?'

A sharp glance of green followed by a placating smile. 'She didn't. Look into my professional records, there's never been a complaint against me.'

They take their leave shortly after, Theo still wondering how 'mistakes' could be prevented from becoming 'complaints' and whether Dr Greene had that power. And then what would happen if she decided to withdraw that protection? On the journey back to the station, he tells Harry he wants her to check out Winters' working background, and, while she is at it, she should look into Gough's as well. She nods. He senses a reservation, asks her to come out with it.

'I don't get it, Sarge,' she says tentatively. 'Thirty years with a bloke, then going off with Eve and Penny. Do people change who they fancy like that?'

Where's this going? I don't want it coming too close. 'Dr Greene and her husband married in 1968. She was only twenty-six, it wouldn't have been as easy to be out as it is today, homosexuality had only just been decriminalised for men.' *Can you imagine that? A mere year before I was born.* Theo holds his shudder in. 'And, yes, I think for some people, gender isn't necessarily that important when it comes to who they fall in love with.'

'I don't think it was about love for Dr Greene. It was about power, being in control. When her husband got to be a renowned academic, she moved on to someone who would be more amenable, docile.' She turns crisply in the car park, expertly manoeuvres into the small space that is left and pulls on the handbrake with a sharp click.

'You could be right.' *Only Penny doesn't come over as a meek, obedient type. Maybe Themis had moved on again, wanted more of an equal. Yes, Penny knows what she is about, is a leader, not a follower.*

Chapter 9

The one and only good thing about Dr Greene's death is that it gives Hannah something to talk about in therapy; she even manages to stretch it over several sessions. And through doing so she begins to appreciate the space Izzie creates for her to say what's in her mind; without self-censoring, almost. The therapeutic space. Hannah has read about it. 'A sacred space,' some worthy has written, and Hannah has been scathing. But now she is getting a taste of that. She supposes others might choose a priest or imam or rabbi for such confession. Only with that wouldn't there come judgement? Judgement with a capital 'J', that is, and punishment? *Ah, and then there would be some kind of absolution.* Hannah keeps waiting for the Judgement and it doesn't come — at least, not in a form she can recognise. However, without Judgement there is no absolution.

'What's the sigh about?' Izzie asks. She has a round face, freckles across a prominent nose, her wheat-coloured hair flecked with silver is cut short as a pixie's. Today the purple she always wears is the shiny varnish on her clipped fingernails.

Hannah considers denying the sigh has any meaning; she hadn't realised it had escaped into the pause. In the end, though, she admits the word which is clanging about her brain like a pinball: 'Absolution.'

Izzie is good at keeping her features neutral and steady. Only this time, there's a flash of something: surprise? Curiosity? 'Absolution from what?'

Hannah is regretting — not for the first time — her frankness. 'I dunno,' she squirms. 'Everything, I suppose. Don't you want absolution?'

Izzie gives one of her non-committal sideways wags of her head. 'What comes to your mind when you say the word "absolution"?'

The dream. Not that the dream is ever far away. Maybe Izzie would like a dream to interpret; even if she's not a Freudian psychoanalyst, therapists like dreams, don't they? And Hannah has an overwhelming desire to give Izzie something which will

60

please her. A titbit, a gift. So Hannah unwraps her dream. The house where she doesn't feel safe, the invaders, the parents who do not hear. Hannah expects Izzie to come back with some wise revelation. Instead the other woman sits for a while, as if still listening for something else, and then says she feels sad and she does manage to look genuinely mournful.

Hannah is aware of her own tears gathering. Apart from directly after 'The Incident', she hasn't cried in a long time and she certainly isn't in the habit of doing it in front of people, and yet her tears are threatening and she doesn't know why. The last time she cried, or rather wailed, she was drunk. It was when Ricky texted her an hour and a half after they were supposed to meet on a date (for the first time without Steff) to say he'd left for New York to start a new job, one she knew nothing about. Then her tears were hot with anger and frustration, now they are cold and persistent as drizzle. 'They don't listen to me, they never have.'

'Who?'

'Mum and Dad. God, what a cliché I am. So, they've always been a little distracted; it doesn't mean anything. It doesn't mean they don't love me.' Pause. 'Does it?'

'Do you feel loved by them?'

'That's a stupid question.' Hannah pulls herself upright and takes tissues. There's a box conveniently placed near the client's chair. The long narrow room is in the upstairs of a converted garage in the garden of a Scalby bungalow. Downstairs the owner offers physio and sports massage. This room, painted with a hint of lavender, is Izzie's domain. It is decorated with large-format photos: one of the coast, one of the moors and one of peacocks in the gardens of an Indian temple. It is furnished with two chairs, a small sofa and low table. 'Of course they love me, they're my parents.'

'That's not what I asked.'

There's a basket of pebbles on the table and Hannah wonders if Izzie lets her other clients play with them. Hannah blows her nose and dabs her eyes, removing mascara and foundation. She must look a sight.

Izzie repeats: 'That's not what I asked.'

'What?' Hannah wants to walk out, flinging those damn pebbles at Izzie. No, no, not at her, just onto the floor. She checks the clock and is relieved to find only five minutes to go.

'I asked, do you feel loved by your parents?'

'I know they love me.'

'There's a difference between know and feel.'

Hannah scrapes her gaze up to Izzie's face. She expects Judgement. Instead Izzie's expression is much as it always is: interested, kind, perhaps a little extra intensely so. 'Yes, yes,' Hannah says quickly. 'I feel loved by them.' *Now will you let me go?*

'You're not breathing, Hannah.'

Hannah exhales loudly. 'I'm fine.'

Izzie takes a big lungful, releasing it long and slow. 'I noticed I was finding it hard to breathe.' She smiles. 'OK. It's the end of the session, same time next week?'

Hannah takes out her purse and offers over her cheque with a resentful flourish. 'You ought to get that looked at. Breathing difficulties, could be nasty.'

'I will.' Izzie's smile deepens. 'See you next week.'

Do I have a choice? Hannah thinks, as she closes the door with a pleasing clack.

Chapter 10

It is Hannah's second week on placement at the GP surgery and Mrs Slater has not returned for a second session. Hannah is greatly relieved and thankful. She remembers the woman sitting down heavily, wheezing after the short walk along the corridor. Her legs, clad in a sheened black stretch fabric, could not close at the knees because of the bulk of her thighs. Her chest and stomach rolled together under the voluminous flowered tunic she was wearing and her numerous rings cut into her short, fleshy fingers. Yet her face was cherubic, round with big blue eyes and a generous pink mouth, at that moment unsmiling, and framed by a neat, fair bob.

She was Hannah's first real client and Hannah felt like a hedgehog with a juggernaut bearing down. She tried to compose herself. 'Mrs Slater, Dr Courtney has suggested we have a chat to see if we think counselling might be a support for you.'

'What I want,' Mrs Slater's voice was shrill. 'What I want is one of them gastric bands. But Dr Courtney won't let me have one unless I speak to you. I'm thinking I might change my doctor anyway.'

Hannah does an elaborate check of the two sheets of paper she is gripping on her lap, not able to comprehend any of it. 'You've been with Dr Courtney for a couple of years?'

'Yes, well, the one before that didn't help much either. Just kept saying I needed to eat less. I hardly eat anything. That's not the problem. It's me genes.' Mrs Slater continued to talk. Hannah was reminded of a car alarm which no-one knows how to switch off. The child's face stuck to the woman's body remained impassive as the mouth moved and words issued forth. Hannah had the sense that she was in danger of being engulfed by this mountain of flesh. It was after a few moments that she realised the lips were still and there was an expectation in the room. She had been asked a question.

'I—I'm sorry, Mrs Slater, what was that?'

The red cupid's bow tautened. 'I said, if I agree to these sessions with you, will I get me gastric band?'

'It doesn't quite work like that, Mrs Slater. The purpose of the sessions would be to explore, explore.' Hannah struggled to find the right sentence construction. 'There are options. We'd be looking at why, what your weight means.'

'I've told you, like I tell everyone, it's me genes, me glands, it's not my doing.' The voice quivered and the child looked about to cry.

Hannah found her revulsion at the other woman's mix of perfume and sweaty body odour turning to fascination of the tremble at subcutaneous fat beneath flawless skin. For a split second she saw the subterranean fault line, a bloody, raw scar, running through the mass of woman opposite her. 'Counselling is not about apportioning blame,' she began quietly, then with more assurance. 'We'll be going on a journey together, Mrs Slater, and what we discover might help you make some decisions for the future. What do you think?'

Mrs Slater had regained control over her voice and countenance. 'If it gets me me gastric band.'

'Fine, good. Now, we've got a few things to go through on this form and then there's a short assessment questionnaire.' They had agreed on another session but Mrs Slater had cancelled during the week. And Craig, Hannah checks the clock, is now officially a 'DNA'. She's more regretful about this and wonders if she had done anything to put him off returning. A tall young man, Craig Parker had no substance to him. He wore a thick black jacket with its hood up and scruffy jeans with a waist which encircled his thighs, revealing shabby underpants. She could hardly see his acne-ridden pale face, long narrow nose with a black ring through one nostril and the dyed-black spiky hair. He'd said little when invited to talk about himself, except that he'd come to please his mam, who thought he wasn't right in the head. There'd not been many words while Craig chewed at what was left of his fingernails and cuticles. Hannah asked him some questions about how he was feeling or had been feeling in the last few weeks and about what he looked forward to or wanted to do with his life now he had left school. He replied with

64

'Dunno' or 'Nothing'. Silence reigned between them. Finally, Craig roused himself. 'I'll be going, then.'

Hannah also shook herself out of her lethargy. 'See you next week, then?'

'You want to?' He didn't turn to look at her. There was a very slight hint of curiosity in his monotone voice and he left with Hannah's assurances that she did indeed want to see him again.

Only he obviously doesn't want to see her. She gets up and opens the top section of the window in the brightly presented consulting room. The cold, metallic, late-afternoon air ambles in. Can't be helped, she tells herself. The main indicator of positive outcomes is the client's own motivation, she'd read that somewhere. She wanders around the room. It has all the paraphernalia of a GP's surgery: desk, computer, filing cabinet, drawers with individually wrapped instruments in, an examination bed behind a striped curtain. She's pulled the chair from behind the table and set it carefully angled by the client's, so they're not face to face, nor quite side by side. In the training room they worked as therapist and client on large floor cushions and she'd wondered about bringing a couple in, only the polished lino looks uninviting.

She sits down again. She's been given various booklets and folders containing policies and guidelines by Dr Courtney, she's flipped through them and put them to one side. She gets out her phone; there's a text from Lawrence suggesting some weekends when he could come up for a visit and asking whether she could set up a drink with Ben. She wishes now she had not told him about her encounter with his school friend as she is fairly sure Ben isn't interested in seeing her since he has not been in touch and she certainly doesn't want to be pursuing him. She replies that any of the dates are fine as her diary is so empty, only could he please come soon. She doesn't add both for her sake and her father's who is becoming daily more cantankerous and will no doubt soften with a visit from his former protégé, the son he wished he'd had. She can leave the Ben question until she knows what Lawrence chooses to do.

The intercom buzzing on the desk makes her jump. After a moment's hesitation she answers it, the receptionist says her next client is here, five minutes early. 'I'll send him down.' It's not a question. Hannah quickly skims through the referral paper: Douglas Olds, fifty-seven, recently given early retirement from his teaching post, married, two grown-up children, no illnesses or recent injuries, average drinker, mild depression, not a suicide risk (*well, he wouldn't be if I'm being allowed to see him*), has had therapy before. She doesn't have time to turn the page to find out more before there's a knock at the door. She sits down and waits. Nothing. Finally she calls for Douglas Olds to enter. He does so tentatively. His demeanour evokes for Hannah all those teachers from her schooldays who were slightly past their best, faces as tired as their crumpled suits and threadbare ties. They were slowly rambling towards retirement and only occasionally burst into any kind of life when a pupil (never Hannah) excelled at the subject the teacher had been obsessively passionate about since the age of eleven. Douglas Olds is more casually dressed, though no less creased, and his mousy hair hangs limply. If the room had been beige, he would have blended in. *Wallpaper man;* Hannah's brain immediately supplies her with the epitaph. She has not brought the forms over from the desk so she has nothing to cling on to or shuffle through; this brings on a moment of panic and she has to focus on settling herself. She wonders if she should get the papers, though she feels paralysed. The seconds appear like hours and she thinks they've probably spent the whole session in this fixed torpor. She looks at the clock — no. Then she remembers the question Izzie first asked her. 'So Mr Olds, what brings you here to me today?'

'She's dead.'

What? The form hadn't mentioned bereavement.

'I didn't tell the other lady.'

Oh, great!

'It sounds all wrong, I used to tell her everything, and now she's dead, and I don't think I can go on.'

Not a suicide risk?

'I miss her terribly.' Douglas Olds' face collapses, his shoulders slump and he is trembling.

Stay with him, Hannah instructs herself. *So Douglas's wife (or lover?) is dead.* In amongst it all, she can catch hold of the sadness.

'And the worst thing is,' he looks up at her fearfully, 'I killed her.'

Metaphorically or really? 'How?'

'With a hammer. I hit her with a hammer, or at least the police think I did. I don't remember doing it. I remember being very angry, really very angry, I don't get angry, Mrs ...? Miss?'

'Hannah.'

'Hannah.' He takes a moment as if he's tasting her name and it's sweeter than he expects. 'I don't get angry, never have ...'

'Everyone gets angry, Mr Olds, there's nothing wrong with anger.'

'Douglas, please. There is when you get so angry that you pick up a hammer and smash someone's skull in.'

Hannah is beginning to feel sick; flashes of Dr Greene's blood-congealed head slip into her mind. *You didn't do it, Douglas, I know you didn't,* she thinks, wishing she could shut him up, but he runs on, with a sleety persistence.

'I don't remember doing it. I remember having a little pick-me-up to get me going, arriving and feeling wonderful seeing her. I loved her, Hannah, I know it was wrong, but I did. And we talked some, like we always did, I felt so safe with her, I could say anything. And then I remember getting angry, not with her, obviously not with her, and she said what you did, "There's nothing wrong with anger, Douglas. Let it out man, let it out." That's the last thing I really recall, everything else is a blur, and I get home and I feel so dirty, and I have a drink and then a shower and I put my clothes in the washer and that's what's got the police saying ... only, I know they are right, they have to be — I killed her.'

Hannah is becoming a suit of armour, all jointed sharp metal. With an enormous effort, she keeps her voice quiet and even: 'Who? Who did you kill, Douglas?'

'Dr Greene, Dr Themis Greene.' Douglas looks up, a lost boy. 'She was my therapist, doesn't it say on my form?'

Hannah wants to scream, wants Douglas out of there. She can't see him, she mustn't see him. Surely it would be unethical. *Fuck,* is the only word that will form itself. The visor comes down. It cuts off her oxygen supply.

Minutes tick by. Douglas is waiting for her to respond and she cannot. Eventually he says in a gentle, teacherly voice, 'Are you OK, Hannah? You don't look well. I'm sorry, I've shocked you. It is shocking what I've said, I understand that. Dr Greene, she was never shocked.' He looks down at his hands.

Hannah cannot fill the void. Without making eye contact Douglas Olds says maybe he'd better be going. Hannah lets out a strange grunting noise and watches him wearily get up and leave, closing the door quietly behind him. Hannah leaps up and dashes to the little sink in the corner of the room. She is not sick, though she thought she might be. She splashes cold water on her face and sucks it into her dry mouth. Finally she stands up, she is shaking. *Fuck, I made a stinking mess of that one, what am I going to do?* She leans up against the desk and takes out her phone. Who should she phone? *The police? Ben? Why him? Orwell?* Yes, of course, Orwell, her supervisor. She dials his number. Gladness yells through her when he answers and says yes, he has a few minutes. 'What's going on, Hannah? You sound all wobbly.' She becomes more so as she explains what had occurred, despite her efforts to give him a factual report.

'I'm really sorry this has happened to you, Hannah, I can hear how upset you are.'

'It's my own fucking fault, I should have read the referral form earlier,' she shouts.

'You're not to blame, you're two weeks into a placement, don't be so hard on yourself. Now, let me see; yes, I have some space, I think it would be good if we book in some time, five-thirty tomorrow? Meanwhile you need to talk to Dr Courtney and see if she thinks it's appropriate to bring in the mental health crisis team for Mr Olds. And, Hannah, you will have to go to the police with this.'

'No, no, I can't,' she wails. 'What about client confidentiality?'

'Doesn't apply with an ongoing murder investigation.'

'But I've seen it, on the TV.'

'Yeah, well,' it sounds like Orwell is smiling broadly, 'you can't believe everything you see on the TV. Is there anyone you can take with you?'

Again her first thought is Ben. 'No,' she tells herself and then realises she's said it out loud.

'No-one? How about one of your fellow trainees on the course?'

She hesitates. 'Agatha, maybe?'

'Sounds like a good plan. You can do this, Hannah.'

Orwell's calmness has begun to rub off on her; she nods, then says yes. He asks her how she is feeling and she replies, 'Like an idiot.'

'Be kinder to yourself, Hannah,' Orwell says cheerily. 'I'll see you tomorrow but ring me later if you need to.'

Once he has hung up, Hannah gets herself a proper drink of water, washes her face, reapplies her make-up and combs her hair. She's ready to speak to Dr Courtney and Agatha. She glances down at the second sheet of Douglas Olds' referral form: all it says is 'Psychotherapist in private practice, three years'.

Chapter 11

The sea is brimful, slopping over its confines onto the land. There is too much water to be contained. The moon is dragging at it, a carpet of indigo. It creeps stealthily until the borderlands become wet, become liquid, become ocean.

****

Aurora is lying on her bed, the sun's heat is falling in a swathe across her face, her chest and her distended belly. She is turning into an aquatic creature, her legs becoming a mermaid's tail in the tepid pool forming around them. The pain of transformation cuts through her abdomen and wraps itself around her spine, a dry, brightly patterned boa constrictor flexing its muscles until it releases its hold again. Before the pain — and there was a time without pain, in that distant land where torture and terror have no abode — Aurora had tried to ring Max, only he hadn't picked up and she'd had to leave a message. She can no longer form words. From somewhere within her depths comes the wailing-grunt of an injured animal.

****

It is a study day on the course and Hannah is supposed to be writing an essay. Instead she is reading Lawrence's latest article online. He characterises Gordon Brown as a man who is drowning, not waving; and too far out to be saved. In a couple of weeks' time the Chancellor will talk about recession and the Brown liner will be effectively sunk; though he will undoubtedly hang on for another year just because he can, despite his lack of electoral legitimacy. His big mistake was to gorge himself on the rosy apple handed to him by Blair, convincing himself that this time it would not be corrupted, while the former PM preened himself, asking, 'Mirror, mirror on the wall, who is the Blair-est of them all?' Lawrence's polemic is fuelled by bitterness; grieving for friends lost in 9/11 and 7/7, he had temporarily changed

70

allegiance from blue to red and written in support of Blair's foray into Iraq, something he now heartily regrets and wants to undo. Hannah clicks the page shut: she is not in the mood for recalling the dead, whether bombed close to her home or close to someone else's.

She prefers to think about yesterday. She had finally given in to James's entreaties to help him with his writing and had met him for a short while before Agatha's birthday meal in the bar of the Thai where they were all going to eat. He was like a puppy, all tail-wagging and panting, which she tried to ignore while talking through how to structure an essay. Finally, when it became too obvious to disregard, she pointed out that he hadn't heard anything she had said. It was then that he grabbed hold of her hand in his surprisingly forceful grip and said he couldn't concentrate, since she has such stunning eyes. Hannah wanted to punch him right in the centre of his pleading smile. Luckily at that point Agatha arrived. James dropped his hold, saying to Agatha that he'd been getting some useful guidance for his essay and then turning to Hannah to add he hoped they could do this again sometime. She made some non-committal noise and gratefully fell into conversation with Agatha and some of her friends who began arriving.

Hannah was determined not to be at the same end of the table as James, even if that meant leaving Tina to his tender mercies, so she snapped up a chair by Clarke. And thankful she is that she did. He was charming and witty and kept them both plied with wine, until, when the party broke up around 9pm, he suggested they both repair to a nearby club. It was loud, garish, beginning to fill up with students; and the shots were cheap. Hannah touches her forehead where an ache still lingers. Clarke knew quite a few people so she was on the edge of many a conversation, she didn't really care, there was laughter and inconsequential chatter. At one point she found herself next to a woman who looked as though she could be underage but was probably in her twenties. Maya, she said her name was. She was very petite, a bit of a goth. Her hair was long, its tips a deep scarlet matching her nails, the rest a glossy witch's cape. She was wearing a tight, long black dress with a cleavage Hannah was envious of and lace fingerless gloves. Maya seemed to know something of Hannah and the connection appeared to have been through Ben. 'Of course, you'd be excused for fancying him, he is an attractive bloke,' Maya said at one point and Hannah agreed, perhaps too fulsomely. (*It was the vodka,* she excuses herself.) Then Maya had arched a slim eyebrow and moved her mouth closer to Hannah's ear, 'Only he does have a girlfriend, you do know that? They're practically engaged.'

Hannah tottered, her gut griped (high heels and vodka, not a good combination). She forced a smile. Leaning away from Maya, she nudged up against Clarke. 'Really?' she said, turning to peck Clarke on the cheek. Luckily he didn't recoil, and instead put his arm around her shoulder where it stayed for a while, long enough for Maya to melt away into the crowd. She hadn't felt like staying after that and had hoped Clarke might walk her home or at least give her a goodnight kiss. He did neither, just said he would see her next week, and she had left unsteadily to go find a taxi.

Her mobile sounds: maybe it is Clarke just woken up from his own morning-after stupor. She stabs at the buttons. It is a message from James. 'Help Hannah having LOADS of problems with my essay. Mayday. James xxx.' She throws down the phone and stomps off downstairs.

****

Douglas Olds is a drinker after all, or at least he's been on a bender recently. Theo can see it in the pink of his eyes and the smell emanating from his pores. Douglas's wife appears unsurprised at her husband's dishevelled state when he finally responds to her calls for him to: 'Come down, the police are here.' In fact she seems unsurprised by everything that is happening, even the police coming to arrest her spouse of thirty-two years. Unsurprised or maybe disinterested. Theo would have liked some histrionics, for Douglas's sake. Instead Mrs Olds helps Douglas on with his coat and asks rather vaguely if she should make up a thermos.

Even with Hannah Poole's new information, Theo has taken several days to get to this point. He would have perhaps left it until the following week. He isn't in the habit of making arrests on Fridays unless absolutely necessary, especially when his friends in Manchester are planning on helping him celebrate his fortieth birthday on the following day. However, the DI has some civic event to attend and is worried about press questions. So Theo is sitting in a nondescript room with DC Shilling by his side, looking across a serviceable table at a broken man. Sitting beside Douglas is the flamboyant Reggie Harvey in tweed jacket and cravat, known for the sob stories he wrings out in mitigation for the most foul-mouthed of antisocial youth. Reggie looks like he has as little appetite for this as Theo. The caution has been given and the tape set going, only Theo doesn't feel like continuing. He momentarily considers handing over to Harry and then realises how unprofessional that would be, so he rouses himself to ask Douglas Olds to go through his story one more time. Of course, it is different from the last time, he knew it would be different, and it is far more confused and rambling and in the end there is the confession, 'I did it, Inspector...'

'Sergeant.'

Douglas doesn't hear the correction; he is weeping, his age-marked hands open on the surface in front of him as if he might suddenly start quoting Lady Macbeth.

Theo sighs, he knows damn well this isn't his murderer and yet what can he do? He begins to gently prod away: where did Mr Olds get the hammer? Did he take it with him with the intention of murdering Dr Greene? What has he done with it? Why didn't they find blood on the shoes he says he was wearing? Normally Theo tries to use holes and inconsistencies in a narrative to prove guilt; here he uses them to try and persuade his suspect of his innocence.

Hannah drinks her coffee standing on the threshold of the French windows opening onto the garden from the kitchen. The air is warm. The sun silvers the green branches of the tree by the fence and catches emerging catkins swaying, a multitude of emerald tongues. She can hear the sea's gentle thwacking, like so many mouths smacking their lips. Her mother is at some fundraising ladies' luncheon. On Hannah's way downstairs, she'd met her father creeping between bathroom and office, wrapped in an ancient blanket dressing gown. She was startled to see the yellow tinge of his skin and smell his sickly sweet odour. But he wasn't interested in her concern or even in her offers of food and drink and he's closeted away once again. The house is being cleaned, the kitchen is already sparkling; as she wanders back upstairs she follows the sound of the vacuum to find Rose preparing the spare bedroom, presumably for Lawrence's visit in a fortnight's time. The stout woman in dungarees, with a long plait of white hair down her back, firmly shuts off the machine and turns, giving a little start at seeing Hannah. Hannah apologises; before either can say more the wall makes a strange sound. It is inhuman and Hannah thinks of a spirit trapped in the bricks. She wonders whether she can divine a presence. There it is again, an unearthly howl from another world.

While Hannah is stayed, Rose is all movement, putting down the vacuum and moving towards the door. 'It's Aurora, poor thing.'

'A gh-ghost?'

The other woman pauses, looking puzzled, then explains slowly, 'Aurora, your neighbour? She's having a baby. Come on.' She's agile for a big woman and quickly leads them both next door. She produces a key from her pocket and thunders in, calling out, 'It's OK, honey, Rose is here, we're coming to help you.' Hannah has only a moment to make connections, having skim-read the address on the van sitting outside. This is Ben's Rose. For some reason this calms her and she is able to start carrying out the older woman's instructions with some efficiency: call for an ambulance; find some clean towels; bring a glass of water for Aurora which she gulps down and partly heaves up again; call Max (this from Aurora). 'Get my husband here,' she whispers through clamped teeth, her body rigid with pain, her face pocked with spots and slick with sweat and her beautiful dark hair knotted and matted. She grabs Hannah's hand. She has no intention of letting it go.

****

Douglas Olds is sweating; it is discolouring his beige shirt. Theo wants him to take off his tie, but it remains stoically tight around his neck. Theo has had enough. The only new bit of information he now has is that Olds occasionally has alcoholic blackouts and may have drunk 'some' before seeing Dr Greene that last time, which hardly helps either Douglas's or Theo's case. Theo halts the interview after fifty-seven minutes and stops the recording, insists Olds says what he wants to eat and drink and sends Harry out for it. He goes upstairs to find Suze and, ensuring that the DI will be absent for some time to come, tells her he doesn't like what he is doing. She is unsympathetic, pointing out that all other lines of enquiry have come to nothing and that he has a confession.

'A confession which won't stand up in court. Douglas Olds will crumble, he doesn't know what he's saying. We'll have to get a psych report done and it'll say he's too confused to stand trial.'

Suze laughs right to her flinty blue eyes. Her brown hair is scraped back today, making her face sharply tooled, its skin sallow and shadowed. 'Too confused to stand trial, that's a new one on me. He'll be found fit, he is fit to stand trial, he'll make his confession in open court, he'll be found guilty. Job done, Theo.'

'And the wrong man in prison.'

Suze shrugs, as if to say it wouldn't be the first time and won't be the last. 'He obviously feels guilty about something. How can you be so sure he didn't do it?'

It's Theo's turn to shrug. 'I just know. If only I could find Eve Cooper or where all that money came from when Dr Greene bought the Centre; there's got to be something else lurking.'

'I wonder what she's called now.'

'Who?'

'Eve. Cooper is her married name, or it was before Greene. She was born ... now, let me see ... yes, I believe she was born a Winters.'

'What? As in Orwell Winters?'

'Now, don't jump to conclusions, there's lots of strands of the Winters family. His great-granddaddy had fourteen children, all of whom got to adulthood and had kids.'

'But Orwell might know Eve?' Theo is beginning to feel some energy coursing through him.

'You'll have to ask him. I'm surprised HOLMES didn't bring that connection in.'

Theo almost kisses her, though he hangs back: there's too many edges to her; his assurance that she is better than any computer will have to suffice.

'And you might like to get in touch with Stephen Poole.'

He pauses on his way out the room, 'Who's he?'

'A financial adviser, lives in York, does lots of work hereabouts.'

'He worked for Greene?'

'How would I know that? All I'm saying is he's the one lots of people go to.'

'And,' Theo's brain is beginning to whirr, 'he's fucking related to Hannah Poole.'

'Language,' Suze says severely.

He can see from her pinched lips she means it. He apologises, then prompts her: 'Is he?'

'Her brother. Now get out of here, I've got my own work to do.'

****

Hannah has never considered the mechanics of childbirth before, and now she hopes she will never have to again. She had supposed that Aurora was having a difficult birth, that there were 'complications' as she had heard muttered of in the past, but Rose assures her everything is as it should be. Hannah shudders. The ambulance is on its way, Max will go straight to the hospital, all they have to do is wait. Aurora's hand is practically breaking bones in Hannah's as another contraction contorts her. Rose chooses this moment to 'pop out for a moment'. Hannah begins to protest, still the other woman goes. The sun-warmed room is becoming unbearably hot as Rose has brought in some extra heaters. Hannah is suffocating. Aurora smells stale, Hannah turns her head slightly; she is terrified the baby will come now while she is alone with this writhing, primal creature.

'There we go, honey.' Rose is back and she has some liquid in a small bottle, which she drops onto a handkerchief to go under Aurora's nose, and she massages a little into Aurora's temples. 'This'll help.'

It does; Aurora grows calmer, her grip on Hannah loosens, she even manages a few words, saying sorry that she's making such a mess of things. She addresses this to Hannah, who would have gracefully accepted the apology; however, Rose responds, telling her she's doing absolutely fine, she needn't worry, everything is going to work out. Hannah gazes out the window at the neatly kept front garden with its crocuses beginning to show their saffron and purple heads. She hears the siren. At last, at last. The tension in her shoulders begins to ease. The paramedics are compassionate and capable, taking over from the two women and efficiently parcelling Aurora into the ambulance. Rose sees them off at the door with more assurances for Aurora. Coming back into the bedroom where Hannah is stuck to the floor, a pillar of salt transfixed by a careless glance, Rose asks if she wants to come in the van with her.

'Where?' Hannah's voice warbles slightly.

'The hospital, of course.'

'Oh no,' Hannah is horrified. She stumbles on, saying something about having to stay in for her dad, who is sick. She feels admonished by Rose's next look and doesn't dare refuse when she is told to clear up in here, even though her stomach twists as she begins to put the sopping blood- and shit-stained towels into a black bin bag.

****

The kindly old crone who came to her rescue with the hazel-eyed dryad washes her forehead with magic potion and Aurora is flying on a carpet of deep-red crimson. There is another woman quite near her being rushed through the afternoon heat in a carriage pulled by screaming horses. She is scared, she is hurting. There's other people around, and noise and light and tubes of plastic and shiny metal, the other woman is told to breathe, to pant, to hold back, to push. She complies as best she can; only Aurora, cocooned in her carpet, can see the despair in her sister's face. Hours pass and fatigue sets in. Aurora knows she must act to help or her twin will turn her face to the wall as her own mother had done more than once. She steps into the body, feels its heavy, damp contours encase her, feels the pain, looks into a man's puce face and tries to remember his name, thinks she ought to have some emotion for him. The body she is in heaves and shudders, an irresistible force goes through her, downwards, and the man suddenly grins, guffaws. A tiny slimy tadpole is fished up from the depths and landed on the pendulous breasts she has inherited from her frightened sibling. It moves. It is still alive. It yawns toothlessly. It wants something from her. Aurora closes her eyes and the tepid salt waters of the India Ocean flood out of them.

Chapter 12

Douglas Olds has had a whole week at home. Theo let him go, still under caution, and has told Hoyle they need to talk to some of Olds' neighbours, cross-check the CCTV. The DI was unconcerned. He told Theo about some out-of-town journalists who had turned up in order to be provoking, but he'd handled them, shut them up with news of Olds being in custody. 'You'll get 'im charged soon, DS Akande,' he'd said on leaving the incident room. Theo calculated he had perhaps a couple of weeks to pursue the Winters connection and talk to Stephen Poole.

Meanwhile, he has had his birthday with his mates (some colleagues from his time in the Manchester force, mostly university pals). Then he'd gone to his parents' home for a party which blended his father's Nigerian roots and his mother's traditions from the more established Cape Verde community in Swansea. He'd felt the bits of himself fitting back together again as easily as in a kaleidoscope after it has been shaken. He knows it is his mother's strength which pins it all together; from stray remarks he knows his father had felt adrift on arriving in Birmingham at the age of eighteen until he had met his soon-to-be wife. Theo returns from all this relaxed if pondering; he has been reminded of what it is like to be with people and in a place where it is not necessary for him to hide a portion of himself. It felt good. He enjoyed himself. Could he settle in a town where this is not possible, might never be possible?

He has DC Chesters with him today, Harry not being on shift. Chesters — tall, sprightly with large ears, and black hair gelled into spikes — makes Theo think of an overexcitable whippet. He is taking his sergeant exams, has big plans to move up the ranks and out of Scarborough which he is keen to share with his superior. Theo misses Harry's reserve and token comments about the weather and the football. They are meeting Winters at the Centre. He lets them in and leads them up to one of the therapy/training rooms. A rectangular space with modestly sized abstract prints in bright reds, blues and oranges on the walls and scented with something mildly spicy. Chesters accepts the offer of a coffee which further irritates his sergeant. When they are finally seated in comfortably padded armed chairs, the two police officers side by side facing Winters, Theo has the momentary image of him and Chesters being there for couples' counselling. The thought makes him want to laugh; he quashes the impulse.

Winters is waiting, apparently at ease. He is wearing a pale-blue shirt with a darker-blue suit with a mandarin collar; his hair and beard are neatly braided. Theo asks him whether he knows Eve Cooper. Orwell replies that he met her at her 'wedding' with Thelma.　　Theo can hear the very faint soft local inflection (against Chesters' more pronounced version) overlaid by the years of trying to hide it. Theo recognises this impulse to cover up: he'd done his best to smooth his own accent into one which would almost pass anywhere. He also picks up Chesters possibly readying himself to crash in, maybe to object to the word 'wedding'. Theo hurries on: 'And you hadn't met her before?'

'Or since.'

'And yet you're related.'

Winters takes longer to respond. Can Theo detect surprise or a tautening of the man's body? 'She was a Winters, or so I understand from talking to her during the wedding party. But there are loads of us Winters, Sergeant; we don't all know each other, even in a small town like this one. Ma was quite selective about the Winters she let into our circle in any case; she blamed Pa's family for everything that went wrong.'

'And you haven't met her since, you say?'

'No.'

Theo can sense a closing-down: Winters won't be volunteering any information about Eve. 'Heard from her, then? A phone call, perhaps, a text, an email?'

'No.'

'You don't know where she is now?'

'I do not.'

Theo is sure Winters is not telling the whole truth. He tries a different tack, asking Orwell what his impression of Eve was.

'Naïve, incredibly so, but then that's how Thelma liked them, so she could rule over them. I would say Eve came across as a kind person, a little fragile perhaps, emotionally. I didn't speak to her for a long time.'

'Long enough to discover you are from the same family.'

'Very extended family, Sergeant Akande. When I introduced myself, Eve said she was a Winters and we worked out we were probably cousins a couple of times removed, or something like that.'

'Do you think she was capable of murder?'

'Eve?' Winters smiles. 'Everyone is capable of murder, given the right circumstances.'

'Except you, or so you said.'

'Yes, I did, didn't I?' Winters' gaze moves up to the ceiling and Theo realises that it has been steadily regarding him since the interview began. Finally Orwell continues with a sigh, 'If someone was physically threatening my girls and hitting them on the head was the only way to stop them, then I'd be able to do that. But Thelma was no threat to me or my family. We'd made our peace.'

'So there was something between you at one time?' Chesters has been champing to say something and comes in with this one.

'Only the usual professional rivalries. You have to understand Thelma liked to have things her way and if she didn't get them her way, she could be ...' he pauses. Then he supplies: 'Difficult. There hadn't been any problems between us in a long while; ask anyone.'

Theo had, or at least he'd had Harry and one of her cronies, a certain Trevor Trench, onto it and they'd turned up nothing of significance. 'What did you think about Eve being a client of Dr Greene's?'

'I didn't know, until she told me how they met.'

This conversation must have been more in depth than Orwell is suggesting, Theo notes. 'And then what did you do?'

'Of course, I was going to put in a complaint but she'd been telling everyone so someone got in before me.'

'Who?'

'I don't know, all these things are kept scrupulously confidential. They weren't technically still therapist and client, so some strings were pulled and Thelma had to do some extra therapy and supervision and meet the ethics committee to say how she had "reflected" on her conduct and that was the end of it.'

'You don't sound happy with the way it was handled.'

Winters sighs. 'I guess in truth we can't control where our lusts will take us, but I don't think Thelma acted well in the matter.'

'You told her?'

A slight hesitation. 'I am ashamed to say, Sergeant Akande, I did not. Maybe I should have done, though I fail to see how that would have resulted in her not being murdered.'

Theo can think of nothing further to say. He tells Winters that if he hears from Eve he must let the police know and the other man says of course he will. Theo sees that Orwell has relaxed considerably and is positively jovial as he sees them out. As soon as they are through the door, Chesters is up and running again. At some point he muses on how bizarre it must be to want to talk to a stranger about all your personal stuff and asks whether the Sarge has ever considered it.

'I have not,' Theo replies and realises once more how easy it is to lie.

Chapter 13

Following the noise of the TV, Hannah finds her mother, as she so often is these days, in the snug. 'Mum.' She has to repeat this a number of times before she gets her attention and can ask her what's the matter with her father. Her mother looks abstracted. Her hair with its weekly spruce up at the hairdresser's is a neat, steely blonde bob; it sits like a wig atop a potholed face. Without make-up her mother's skin has the texture of a dishrag which has been wrung out too often, her thin lips turned permanently down to join deep creases either side of her chin. Her eyes are pale and glassy. She is wearing a velour tracksuit which was new in the '80s. Hannah repeats her question.

'Nothing, dear, he's taken Lawrence to the newspaper office to show him round.'

Probably to the great irritation of the present editor and staff. 'I know that, Mum, only lately he's been looking frail and acting strange.' Though Lawrence's arrival the previous evening has perked him up considerably, as it has her.

Her mother turns back to the TV. 'Has he, dear? It's probably a bit of flu.'

'I don't think so, Mum … Mum!' The baby's cries from next door start up again. They have been a constant background track on this side of the house for, it must be, nearly three weeks. Hannah wonders how Aurora can stand it. Val Poole retrieves the remote and turns up the TV volume, then sips from her sherry glass. Her daughter turns away in disgust, shouting over her shoulder as she leaves that she's going out, to supervision.

She has a bike. Agatha was going to consign it to the tip when Hannah had claimed it. She spent Sunday getting it into working order with instructions downloaded from the internet. An hour in she had been on the point of giving up on the whole enterprise, especially as she had already broken most of her nails, but she had persevered and got it running. And now she has some transport of her own. With pride she wheels it round to the road and sets off. She is wearing leggings with a knee-length apricot tunic topped with a long knitted cardigan and scarf as it is chilly when she picks up speed. She has her hair held back in a large clasp and has dispensed with most of her make-up. She feels light, as if she is flying, as she pedals along the Esplanade; the sea is dazzling, the trees greening as she passes.

She had persuaded Clarke to meet with her on Saturday night. It had been a disastrous evening. They had bickered over who should pay for the meal; she thought he should and he wanted her to go halves. They had bickered over which film to see and she had finally agreed to see his choice, a fantasy full of special effects and with no discernible plot. There had been none of the furtive 'accidental' moments when shoulder would press against shoulder or skin would stroke skin, which Hannah had ached for; and Clarke had allowed her to walk home on her own, abandoning her without ceremony and no more than a half-hearted 'See you.' Of course, he could be shy, hiding it under his tough exterior; Hannah suspects he might be. Maybe she should give him another chance.

Orwell makes her a cup of coffee before leading her up to his therapy/training room, which smells to Hannah of Lawrence's kitchen when he's making simnel cake. Orwell says she's looking fresh and rosy and she beams until she hears it in Steff's voice and it becomes much less pleasing. They sit down, he invites her to start and Hannah hears the thump of stony ground meeting feet; she has to admit to Douglas still being in the forefront of her mind and, despite all Orwell's best efforts, she still feels responsible. 'I know what you'll say,' she rushes on. 'He's not my responsibility, I shouldn't have been put in the position of seeing him, only I was, I did see him and speak to him, well, he spoke to me, rather, and I was stupid, stupid, I couldn't think of anything to say. I should have known what to say. And then going to the police, it feels all wrong, the paper says they've arrested him, that's all my doing. I feel so, so bad,' she finishes weakly, wrapping her arms around her. She's cold. She pulls her cardigan back on.

There's a pause before Orwell says, 'You must be a powerful person.'

'Wha-at?'

'To wield that much influence over North Yorkshire Police as to force them to arrest the wrong suspect.'

Hannah is nonplussed. 'It must have been what I'd said that made them do it.'

'How do you know?'

'I made a statement and they immediately bring Mr Olds in.'

'You make a statement and three days later they arrest Mr Olds.'

It's like talking to a wall. Hannah despairs. She looks down; her hands are clenched together. Orwell waits and then asks what is going on. 'You're not listening to me,' she throws at him.

'What tells you I'm not listening to you?'

Hannah stutters and blusters. She can't find the correct phrasing. In the end she says that he's always contradicting her, knowing how foolish that sounds.

Another gap before he responds gently, 'OK, OK, Hannah, let's just accept that you feel this is your fault, that you believe you have the power to push the police into action. Let's sit with that for a moment.'

This is even worse. Hannah's discomfort detonates through her body and into her mouth. 'No, no, I don't want it. I don't want it to be my fault, I want you to stop it being my fault, I don't want it, take it away.' She looks up at him, then quickly away at the blasts of colour on the wall.

Ponderous and softly spoken as ever, he says, 'Wow, that's a reaction.'

She feels idiotic and tells herself to calm down and shut up.

'Now I'm guessing you're reproving yourself, Hannah. I'd rather you congratulated yourself even if that's hard to do. You do put me in a tough situation, however: on the one hand you want me to take away your feeling of being at fault and on the other hand every time I offer you another perspective which absolves you, you reject it.'

'I know, stupid.'

'Try saying "interesting" instead of "stupid". We're only beginning to learn about each other and how to be in relation to each other; everything that happens is useful in this process. I understand right now you feel a huge sense of responsibility and this feeling is very upsetting for you. That's how you feel and that's OK. You might like to wonder in therapy about other times you have felt a huge sense of responsibility and felt upset. In this moment I'd like you to try and take on board that I have a different perspective. I do not hold you responsible for the state Douglas Olds is in nor for the procedures of the North Yorkshire Police. Is this a stance you're prepared to consider?'

She nods. She doesn't trust herself to put into words all the clashing phrases which are knocking at the inside of her skull. When Orwell asks her if she wants to say more, she shakes her head, so he suggests they move on. 'You said you had a new client, a private one. Tell me about them.'

With an effort she puts her mind to Darren Frost and recounts how 'D' (as she refers to him to Orwell) had phoned her up having found her name on the Centre's website, and she had arranged an assessment session. A man of average height and build with dark hair and tanned skin, Darren Frost is thirty-two years old and sells photocopiers, and disconcerted Hannah by calling her 'sweetheart' until she corrected him. 'Oh, wash my mouth out,' he had said, putting fingers with manicured nails to his mouth in a stagey attitude of prudishness. Hannah was really beginning to dislike him and also wondering why he was there: apart from a broken marriage and not being able to see much of his little girl (now five) there didn't appear to be a lot of unhappiness in Darren's life. Then he'd eagerly looked around the room. 'Was this the place?'

'Sorry?'

'Where you found the body? The crime scene, like?'

The room had appeared to shift. Hannah had half wanted him to repeat it: she thought she must have got him wrong, only he was sitting there expectantly. 'Pardon?'

'I read it in the paper. Your name was in there, and when I saw you on the website I knew I had to see you. Bit of a celebrity?'

'Really?' Hannah wanted to yell at him to fuck off and get out; instead she said she needed a few more of his details, filled in the last of her assessment form and somehow took his money before telling him she would be in touch. In supervision Hannah expects Orwell to advise her to get rid, Darren is a slime. On the contrary: Orwell is fascinated.

'I'm glad you find him noteworthy,' Hannah says crossly. 'He makes my skin crawl.'

'I wonder how he experiences his own skin.'

'You're not seriously suggesting I carry on seeing this man?'

'That is, in the end, up to you, but you didn't blow him out at the time, so what was it that stopped you from doing that?'

'I need the clients,' she says, only half truthfully.

'Anything else? Think back: was there a moment that piqued your curiosity?'

Hannah considers. 'Maybe the moment when he talked about his little girl; he did seem genuinely attached to her.'

'So there's something you could work with him on.'

'He came to me as a voyeur, to pry, for some kind of sick thrill.'

'Maybe, or perhaps he feels like a voyeur in his life, shut out in some way? He was already looking at the list of therapists on the website when he saw your name and made the connection; he was already looking for help. And any number of people will have read that article, will come to you knowing what happened; they just might not be as upfront about it.'

'You're telling me to work with him?'

'I'm telling you not to dismiss working with him. Think about it.'

'I'm not going to do it.'

Slowly Orwell smiles. 'OK, that's fine, you've made that decision, you must know that you can always say no.'

They finish shortly afterwards, Hannah, still irritated, determined to tell Darren Frost to find another therapist.

Chapter 14

Where is he? Max had assured her he'd be home after his 'very important meeting he simply had to attend' so they could have lunch together. She's even managed a shower and to get dressed in honour of this promised delight. She strokes her hands across the soft linen of her turquoise geometrically-patterned skirt. It just about fits with the buttons at the waist left undone. As she shifts her weight the wicker chair creaks. Max had bought her the chair with its extravagant fanned back, when she had announced she was pregnant. He had said it would be kept close to the bed so that she would only have a short distance to go when the little chap needed a feed. She herself had had a vision of sitting in it, dressed in a long white cotton nightdress with a cashmere shawl around her shoulders. Her arms, the posture of her whole body, a snug cradle for her new baby, his creamy cheek against her breast and his pink lips forming a kiss as he suckled contentedly before peacefully drifting off to sleep.

Now the nightdress is so stained with vomit and leaking milk that it is a rag under the kitchen sink and the shawl has been thrown. The chair has hardly been used for its designated purpose. Oliver makes such a fuss whenever he feeds, butting his dark head into her chest as if he means to hurt her and smacking his fat red lips as he draws forcefully on her nipples. Then he needs to be walked up and down and winded over and over before he finally cries himself into a comatose state. After the second night Max had complained he was suffering from sleep deprivation and Aurora took herself and the baby off to the back room downstairs.

This had been their dining room. It contains a glass-topped table surrounded by slender-legged maple-wood chairs, a tall vase filled with dried grasses and seed heads sprayed silver and a metal lamp which splays soft light upwards and across the ceiling. All these Aurora has pushed together into the corner the furthest away from the window, where she has replaced them with a length of yellow swirl-patterned carpet across the pine flooring and an old battered rocking chair she had discovered in a local second-hand shop. The gentle backwards-and-forwards motion seems to encourage Oliver into a less frenetic frame of mind. Meanwhile, Aurora hooks her toes into the rough warmth of the carpet as she looks out on the dark garden. In the light she knows she would see a gravel path meandering between weeded flower beds to a round gazebo nestling between cherry trees which will flower pink very soon. Only the night is populated with shape shifters. Any ambient light touches on the steely, curving blades of the sea hollies, an army of samurai scimitars marching across the garden. With their leaves gone, the trees stretch their branches into the sky in sacrifice. At their feet the arendsii bow their cowled heads and murmur prayers for the dying, which Aurora has come to believe are as much for her as she sits with an alien creature sucking her dry. Oliver reaches up and punches her on the chin, hard enough to leave a red mark. She had fallen asleep again. For a moment she has no idea what she was doing. The child she was holding was not hers. It couldn't be. This dark-skinned changeling, with black hair and jagged nails. She has no memory of becoming a mother. Perhaps it was just another illusion.

Max arrives, he bends to kiss her and finds only her cheek.

'You're late,' she says. Does he smell faintly of wine?

'Hardly.' Max is pulling off his buttercup-yellow tie and shirt, asking after someone called Oliver.

'Oliver?'

He pauses, a rugby shirt ready to go over his head. 'What's happened?'

She smoothes out her skirt across her thighs and knees. 'Nothing. Oliver's fine. He's sleeping.'

He wants to know for how long, whether he should go and feed him before they eat or leave him for a while. She shrugs. She has the feeling there is something vital she has forgotten and scrapes round her mind to try and discover it.

'Aurora.' Max's voice is loud behind her.

She turns to find him standing there with a large child in his arms.

'Aurora, he's soaking, he's been crying, he must have been awake for ages.'

She shakes her head. 'I didn't hear him wake.' Her hands hold on tightly to each other. She had heard a baby yelling, but it hadn't been Oliver, it was another baby, she would have known if it was her own. Everyone says you can recognise your own baby's cries in a crowd.

Max bounces the grizzling Oliver on his hip, looking his wife up and down. 'I'll go and change him.'

'Max.' He pauses and she says croakily, 'Do I look OK?'

He doesn't look over his shoulder as he leaves. 'Yeah.'

Chapter 15

The trees gramp their way up the slope, bowed forward, mountaineers shuffling into a headwind. Dark branches naked against the blue sky — elder, rowan, hornbeam, hazel; Rose has been tutoring Hannah. She had persuaded Hannah to buy some bedding plants to 'cheer up Mrs Poole'. Val had handed over gardening duties to Rose some years back though sometimes wistfully regards her former domain from the kitchen French windows. Rose had told Hannah about the aspen as they dug by its side. 'It'll cool a fever and its leaves shiver with all the forgotten truths there are to tell.' Hannah finds Rose's magical thinking faintly amusing as well as strangely comforting. Anyway she's a quick learner and now knows her blue tit from her chaffinch and, as she looks out across the bay, the skittish little sanderling from the orange-stockinged oystercatcher. Overhead the herring gulls are staking out their territories with screeches and puttering laughs.

She and Lawrence have paused halfway up the winding cliff path. He agreed to come on her daily stomp (it's cheaper than the gym, she explained). They have gone down to the beach and are heading back along one of the rickety ways through the once-kempt Victorian gardens. There's a hint of wild garlic in the air. Lawrence doesn't look entirely comfortable in his long, tailored woollen coat and shiny shoes. He is cold, his skin pale and his stout nose and ear tips reddening. Hannah had offered him a knitted hat, which he had refused, looking askance at the rainbow-coloured affair she put on. She had laughed, saying Scarborough was the realm of ridiculous hats, pointing out examples as they strode together beside a sea brushed white by a teasing wind.

Lawrence had commented that she seemed more relaxed on their walk. *Than when?* she wonders. *Than at her parents' house, certainly.* He asks her whether she is enjoying seeing clients more than when she first started. She replies in the affirmative, wanting to say more but knowing she cannot. She would have liked to tell him about the return of Craig, how she had taken in a pack of cards (at Orwell's suggestion) and now they played endless games of whist and rummy and 21 while they talked; or rather, she offered up thoughts and suggestions about life in general and being a teenager in particular and he agreed, disagreed or said, 'Mebbe.' She noticed he liked to win but didn't like it when she let him. He kept promising to show her a trick 'Gramps', his father's father, had taught him. She asked him about his granddad and he had replied flatly, 'He's dead.' He refused to be drawn further. Then there was Elsa, a gregarious, pretty woman in her mid-thirties, who was frequently off work with a bad back and migraines which had no discernible physical cause. In amongst her chatter, Elsa had described a pattern of bad relationships which she was eager to avoid repeating. And Hannah had thought ruefully, *Tell me about it*. Finally, there was Darren. She had rung him with the intention of telling him to find another therapist and had heard herself agreeing to six sessions. This week she had summoned up all her confidence to tell him that they would work better if he could stop trying to flirt with her. He had looked embarrassed and then told her angrily that she was mistaken, he wasn't behaving any different with her than he would with anyone else. He left still peeved, his mouth pinched and his goodbye curt. She wonders if he will come back.

Panting a little, she and Lawrence reach the top of the cliff and the Esplanade with its displays of sun-dipped primulas and dwarf daffodils. *You could fall in love with this place. You could fall in love here.* However, perhaps not with Clarke after all, even though he might still provide a diversion, and not with Ben either. It seems she has been specifically excluded from the gathering Lawrence is off to later to catch up with his old schoolmate. They pause a moment. Lawrence scans the horizon, where sapphire sky dips into cobalt water. He appears even more uneasy; perhaps it wasn't only the tramp they've had. She asks him what's on his mind and he tells her he's worried about her father.

'I know he's not been well lately,' Hannah says slowly, not wanting anything to spoil the lightness she is feeling.

He hooks his arm through hers and says gently that he thinks it's serious, that she and her brother should try and talk to him.

'Stephen's away, a fortnight in the Maldives or something. Anyway, Dad's more likely to tell you than either of us.'

He hesitates and she guesses Stan Poole has told him something. He won't admit it; he swiftly leans forward and kisses her on her forehead. 'I'll speak to him before I leave.'

Once they're back at the house, Lawrence goes to get changed and Hannah offers to make her parents a meal. Her father says he'll eat soup and a sandwich in his office, while her mother does the same in front of the TV. Hannah eats hers in the kitchen proofreading her latest essay, an exploration of relational concepts from the point of view of various therapy modalities. By the time Lawrence is ready to leave she's finished her work and washed up. He's looking sharp in his raw silk-shirt of the palest blue, navy lined waistcoat and Savile Row trousers. He's probably too sharp for Scarborough; she doesn't tell him this, instead says he's looking good, knowing how he can lack confidence in his appearance before a social event.

Max has been assigned the role of getting Lawrence to the right bar in town and as she accompanies Lawrence to the front gate, they meet Max coming in the other direction. He is more dishevelled than usual, his jacket an old anorak and his trousers recently stained with food, then hastily wiped. However, he gives them both a hearty greeting and a grin which doesn't quite make it to the rest of his face. Then he begins to trip over his words and Hannah only slowly gathers that he's asking her for a favour. His round cheeks are rouged when he finally comes to a halt with, 'She asked if you'd go in and stay with her. I won't be able to go else.'

'Aurora? Asked for me? We hardly know each other.'

His expression is beseeching, he adds quickly that he'll only be gone a couple of hours and that the baby is fed, washed and sleeping, finishing, 'But, if you're busy?'

Busy? Of course she isn't. She shrugs and says she will. *Why not?* She can manage two hours' babysitting, she tells herself. When she arrives next door, she quickly realises it's Aurora she's minding. The woman is a mess, dressed in jogging pants, sweatshirt and dressing gown; her unwashed hair is an uncombed heap collected together in a large grip away from her wan face, which is all puffy pouches and oily shadows. She doesn't acknowledge Hannah's arrival into the lounge or her greeting; she is perched on the edge of the sofa staring into the bassinet where Oliver sleeps, a blanket tucked up to his chubby chin. Hannah sits in the armchair and joins Aurora in her vigil. The baby's fingers clasp and let go the edge of the blanket, he yawns, eyes screwed shut, and then he is still again apart from his almost imperceptible breaths.

'Will he be alright?' Aurora says finally, her voice dull.

'He looks fine to me. Has he been ill?' Thus starts a stilted exchange with Aurora lapsing into silences and appearing to forget Hannah is there, before suddenly starting up again with her odd, monotonal questions. She wants to know who Oliver belongs to. Who brought him here? (Hannah wonders if these are spiritual or existential queries.) Can Hannah see that he's been swallowed up? Hannah does her best to come up with responses though it's hard to gauge whether the other woman is taking much notice.

'I'm afraid,' Aurora says after one of her long pauses during which Hannah checks the clock and sees that thirty minutes have gone by. She's feeling stiff and thirsty in the over-heated room.

'Of what?'

'Him.' Aurora points at Oliver who is snoring quietly.

Hannah takes a guess. 'Of hurting him? I imagine many new mothers are.'

'Of him hurting me,' Aurora says bluntly, finally looking Hannah in the eye.

Hannah winces at the other woman's bloodshot stare. 'I don't think — I mean, he's too little.'

'Max hurts me.' Aurora rubs her arm.

'Does he, does he? What do you mean "hurts"?' Hannah has to root herself in the chair or she'd be out the door.

Aurora speaks over her. 'He's not my husband, you know. Max left weeks ago.'

Into this next hush, Hannah suggests as gently as she can that maybe Aurora should talk to someone, her GP, get some help. Tears begin to seep from Aurora's eyes, she hugs herself ever tighter until she squeaks out that she thought Hannah was there to help.

'I am, I am, of course, look, how about I get us both a cup of tea?' She feels foolish even as she says it.

Then Aurora collects herself, wiping her face, saying she's been talking nonsense because she's so tired, and what an awful host Hannah (the first time she has used her name) must think her. She'll get the tea and she made some cake this afternoon, she'll bring it in. She takes an inordinately long time in the kitchen, so Hannah looks round the room. As well as the suite covered in brown cord, there's a TV, bookshelves and wicker occasional tables. There's some watercolour prints of places up the coast on the dove-grey walls. After inspecting them, Hannah begins to tidy, putting magazines in the wicker rack and reshelving the strewn books (which, she gathers, are normally kept in alphabetical order by author). There's a box for the toys, left where they've fallen. On one of the tables she finds a stack of paper, torn into careful ten-centimetre squares. On each is the word 'Help'. Aurora bustles back in with a tray and Hannah quickly takes her seat again. Aurora is chattering now, about the weather, about wanting to go back to work, about Blair having to stand down.

'He did.'

'When?' She looks shocked.

'Two years ago.'

'Yes, I knew that, I meant the other one, what's his name?'

'Brown.' Hannah is finding out that the tea is cold and the cake appears to be made from pure rock salt. She puts down her mug and plate. 'Look, Aurora, I bet you're done in, why don't you go and have a nice long bath? I'll stay here with Oliver.'

'Oliver?' She looks around.

'Your baby.'

'I knew that.' The flat tone is back and her body is slumped.

Hannah takes another look at the sleeping child and wonders if pricks from spindles might have been involved. No matter: he is slumbering contentedly and she knows he can scream when he wants anything, so she can focus on his mother. Aurora has lost all volition and meekly follows instructions from Hannah, to get undressed, to get into the bath that's been drawn for her, to lie back with her head above the water and listen to the music. The bathroom is in a relatively good state: Rose is still employed on a weekly basis here. While checking in on both Oliver and Aurora, Hannah collects laundry and puts on a load. She also washes up the crockery from the lounge and what's been left in the kitchen. She disposes of the cake and makes her and Aurora a hot chocolate, which she insists the other woman drinks before she puts her in a clean nightdress and tucks her into bed. Aurora is almost immediately asleep. Back in the lounge Oliver is still snoring. Hannah settles down into her chair with a Ruth Rendell from the bookshelf and waits for Max.

The house remains peaceful until he returns, some three hours after he left. He is full of apology and also thanks, eventually, hesitantly asking if everything had been OK. When Hannah nods he looks disbelieving. She asks him if Aurora has seen her GP lately and he is immediately on guard, replying that the health visitor has been. 'What's happened?' he wants to know, glancing over at his son.

'Nothing,' she says soothingly. 'I just think Aurora could do with some support.'

'She hasn't been getting much sleep, neither of us have, that's normal, and,' he gives her a sideways inspection, 'she's got a vivid imagination, always has had.'

'I know having a baby is tough, only I think Aurora needs ...' Under his scrutiny she loses some assurance, mutters that since she's been doing this counselling training—.

Max jumps in: 'She's not mad!'

'I didn't say she is. She could maybe do with some more help, that's all.'

'Rose comes in once a week, cleans, does the garden, and I'm at home a lot.'

Hannah gives up: it's not her problem after all. She says she'd better be getting home, asks if Lawrence came back with him.

Max shows her out. 'No, Ben wanted to see a band and Lawrence and Theo went along for the ride.'

'Theo? Theo Akande? Detective Sergeant?'

Max nods, adding what a nice bloke Lawrence is. He pulls open the front door and then won't let her exit; he grumphs, 'Hannah, thanks for tonight, I really appreciate it and I know Aurora does too. I'm sure she'd like you to call by sometimes, she likes your company.'

'She doesn't know me.'

'Please, Hannah, she needs all the friends she can get,' he says quietly, letting her go out into the chilled night.

Chapter 16

Hannah is watching Clarke, appreciating his litheness. His diminutive, slender body is taut, a black-sheathed wire wound tight between transistors. His black hair is cropped, prickling upwards; he has already tanned in the weak spring sun. She wonders why he has not responded to her last few texts, carefully worded to be witty, self-deprecating and not too needy. He is not looking at her. Indeed it could be said that he is scrupulously ignoring her. Hannah is becoming increasingly anxious to prove this hypothesis wrong now that it has occurred to her. She would like to catch his attention, share a moment together of irritation at James (who is holding forth again) with a surreptitiously raised eyebrow. Only Clarke is gazing at James, and if Hannah didn't know him better she would have to admit Clarke has a sympathetic expression on his face.

Finally, finally Clarke turns towards her but it is not with intimacy or even kindness. Then Hannah realises that everyone's eyes are on her. The bland room trimmed in terracotta and navy becomes hotter and stuffier, she feels the flurry of phantom bird wings trapped inside her ribcage. 'What?' she asks, clumsy and stupid; she hasn't been following the proceedings.

James re-doubles his sorrowful expression. They've already all been in trouble for missing the 20th of April, his birthday. *Why tell them eleven days later?* He lets his head sink between his shoulders. It is Clarke who speaks for him. 'James sent you a text asking for help with his essay and you never replied.'

Hannah tries to dredge it all up from her memory: *had he?* She recalls that meeting when he had said that ridiculous thing about her eyes, tried to grab her hand; was there anything after that? She begins to say she doesn't think so. James interrupts, telling her the date and the time. *How can he remember that?* He sounds whining to her; the others, though, appear to be taking him very seriously, especially Clarke. He leans forward, his leg jitters up and down, he starts to tell her off; yes, really: she can hardly stomach it. Clarke is telling her how she should be more responsive, more considerate to James as she knows the difficulty he has in asking for help. After the tirade she points out, mustering some force into her tone, that she had helped, had spent time with James before Agatha's dinner. 'And James ... James ... he ...' She turns away from Clarke to the other man. 'You ... you ...' She catches sight of a secretive smile on James's dipped face. 'You came on to me,' she finishes crossly. There's a hushed collective gasp and Hannah straightens, for a moment triumphant. Only for a moment.

Clarke laughs harshly. 'Came on to you Hannah? I doubt it. James wouldn't have the guts. You came on to him more like, that's your style, and he rebuffed you. Is that why you've been ignoring him? Can't bear to be rejected? Is that your problem, Hannah?'

She's got his attention and she doesn't want it. She thought he liked her; why is he being so unkind? She looks to the others, Agatha and Tina, for some sisterly support and doesn't find any; their faces are closed to her. She turns to Fred. *Surely he must see how unfair all this is? He must intervene?* Fred is sitting back in his chair, his expression impassive, maybe even a little amused, his hands clasped across his round belly. The sun has not been kind to his raw skin and bulbous nose. She thinks about defending herself and then a sense of pointlessness drains through her, leaving her empty. No-one in that room is on her side, no-one will believe her. She stares at Clarke for a moment and suddenly fears what he might say about the texts she has sent him. She shrugs. She slouches. She focuses on her finger's cuticles, thinking maybe she should have a manicure soon.

Tina and Agatha both say they stand ready to help James in his struggles with his essays and Agatha talks about how sometimes she finds it hard ('You, Agatha?' James improvises a mix of surprise and obsequiousness) because she always wants to get things just right, perfect, even in the first draft. At moments Hannah peeks at Clarke. He has his back half-turned to her. She wants to go over and grab him and make him listen to her, make him understand; it wasn't her, it wasn't her fault. The effort of staying still and unobtrusive brings an ache into her shoulders which then begins to ease its way down her back to vice her spine in its clutches. Fred calls time and disappears, the others follow more slowly, Tina stopping to ask whether Hannah wants anything. Hannah can only just manage a stiff shake of her head.

Alone she thinks about leaving. *I don't have to stay. I don't have to put up with this. Fuck them all, I don't need them.* She picks up her bag ready to go, only her cramped legs are not cooperating. If she exits now, she couldn't come back. If she didn't come back, she would have failed again, proving her father (and Lawrence) right about her lack of staying power. If she didn't come back she would have to give up the course and stop seeing Izzie. She wants to leave. She can't leave. She feels trapped in a sticky web of consequences. She pulls out her phone and texts: 'Clarke, what was all that about? CSL. Hx.' Then she presses 'send'.

Chapter 17

Texts are a treacherous drug. They promise instant gratification but never deliver.

01:05:09   18:00

Hi Clarke, how's it going? Strange day 2day. What was all that stuff about in group process? ASL. Hx

01:05:09   19:00

Hey Clarke, guess ur busy? Seriously though, what were u talking about in GP? Get back 2 me, H x

01:05:09   19:45

Hey, u got ur phone off? I don't think so. Look I know I've not been that nice 2 James at times, but u said urslf he's a bit of a pain and I DID help him with his f**king essay. HMU.

01:05:09   19:55

And ur not replying WHY? Come on Clarke, ur making me anxious, thought we had something good between us. H x

01:05:09   20:03

OK, enough game playing, TEXT ME.

01:05:09   20:10

What so now James has got more precious feelings than I have? U'd get back to him pretty sharpish, but oh no, can't be arsed with me. JUST TELL ME WOT'S GOT IN2 U.

01:05:09 20:15

Bet you're ving a fucking good laugh at me, Clarke, with ur new best mate James. DILLIC.

01:05:09 20:17

Oh and another thing, James did come on2 me, he's a lying bastard if he says otherwise. Said he was distracted by my beautiful eyes and grabbed my hand. What's THAT if not coming on to me? Do me a favour, me come on2 James? Credit me with a bit more taste.

01:05:09 20:20

u can do wot u like Clarke Stone, say wot u like to the others, but uve no balls if u cant even reply to me.

01:05:09 20:22

u know wot, get out of my life, Clarke. DON'T BOTHER TO REPLY NOW.

02:05:09 03:33

Can't sleep, Clarke, u must ve got my txts by now. Please Clarke, ve sme compassion, jst let me know ur OK, am worried about u. Sry if i went off on 1, u know I dnt mean it. H x

Chapter 18

Officers have trawled through the available CCTV recordings, but the crossroads where the Scarborough Centre for Therapy Excellence sits is not well served. The building does not have any of its own. There's footage from the mini-supermarket which adjoins it, the post office and betting shop which are across one road in the southerly direction and the pub which is opposite in the easterly direction on the way to the sea. None of this reveals anything except that Penny Greene did leave Dr Greene to work, as she said she had, a good thirty minutes before Winters and Gough vacated the building and Olds arrived. Theo has ordered CCTV images covering a wider area to be checked by reluctant detectives who are fast becoming gritty-eyed from staring at grainy animated pictures. So far this has only unearthed an unreported brawl between a couple of local ne'er-do-wells, which everybody would rather ignore.

Theo has also learned from Gough that the Centre has a back entrance. Furthermore (because he's done it under Suze's direction) he knows it's possible to get a long way without showing up on any CCTV cameras by using it in conjunction with various snickets. Only certain people had keys for the back door: Greene (who had left hers at home, thus giving Penny access), Gough, Winters and a cleaner with a very good alibi. Theo rolls the three around in his mind. Gough doesn't seem the type to sneak through dark alleyways. *If Gough had done it, he would have gone in through the front door and then coolly justified it to anyone prepared to listen once he was finished. Winters is undoubtedly hiding something, but a murder?* Theo is unconvinced.

He is equally confused by Penny Greene. Her story stacks up and she gives the appearance of grieving. However, it does feel to him like a performance. She was once something of an actress, or maybe all thespians come over as always playing a part? In addition, she seems less than interested in the investigation and in the killer being tracked down. It's been over ten weeks since Dr Greene was found dead, seven since Olds was arrested and then released. Why hasn't the path to his door been beaten bare by the feet of Penny Greene? Why haven't there been any complaints from her about the slowness of progress and the lack of charges? Every time he sees her, she talks sympathetically about the complexities of the case and how Themis (she never fails to call her this, and Theo wonders about the existence of more intimate pet names) wouldn't want anyone wrongfully accused. Take your time, Sergeant, take your time, I'm in no hurry; this message whispers through her words and attitude. It's not one he's come across before in his career from those affected by crime.

Yet there is nothing to connect her to her partner's death. Her phone and computer, which she willingly yielded, gave up nothing beyond the ordinary. Even so, pay-as-you-go phones and roving email addresses can be bought, set up and ditched without much trouble if you're organised. Just as the ever-elusive Eve has successfully discarded the only phone connection they had to her. Dr Greene's electronic paraphernalia (of which there was a perplexing array) did expose a dalliance (which Penny said, again pretty convincingly, she knew about) with a (male) professor living in the Czech Republic who she hooked up with at various conferences. Plus some smart movements of money which fell into the category of tax avoidance rather than fraud.

Theo is sitting in the reception area for Stephen Poole's office. True, Poole shares it with four other professionals — another financial adviser, a solicitor and two architects — but it's certainly a plush space in a swanky York address and the receptionist has served him and Harry with real coffee and shortbread biscuits. Stephen is keeping them waiting for their appointment. Theo checks his phone: there's a brief text from Lawrence suggesting some dates for Theo to visit London. Was this the beginning of something, perhaps, dare he say it, a relationship?

He remembers Lawrence easing up as the evening progressed and them sharing their interest in food, metropolitan travel, football and (strangely) 'X Factor' (Ben ridiculing the latter). Theo felt their mutual attraction; he liked the way Lawrence looked, though he couldn't be said to be his usual 'type'. Broader, bigger, older than the men he habitually went for. *Yet nothing had really worked out in the past, so maybe these differences are a good thing? And what am I to make of his texts since he returned home? Regular, yes, but hardly forthcoming; for a writer he doesn't waste his words.* On the other hand *(Am I on my fourth hand by now?)* Lawrence is unshakeable in his determination to get Theo to go and stay with him. He's not accepted any avoidance strategies: lack of time, would the summer be better? Perhaps when there's something on they both want to go to? Over the weekend, Theo attempted to pin down Ben to get his advice, but he was at some mysterious wedding or other. *'Rite', did Ben use that word? What is he into?* Theo is beginning to sort through the dates against his diary when a buzzer sounds on the receptionist's desk and they are told they may go in to see Mr Poole.

A door regulated by the receptionist opens onto a carpeted corridor of doors, each announcing in brass letters the name and profession of the occupant behind it. One door has been thrown open and Stephen Poole is waiting for them. He has a large office, tidy, a vast mahogany desk taking centre stage. Poole seats himself behind it and indicates two armchairs opposite him for Theo and Harry. The room's window has a view of the minster and trees beginning to burst into pinky May-time blossoms which remind Theo of a disastrous hat his elder sister once wore to a wedding. Stephen's desk has photos of a slim woman and a couple of smartly dressed pre-teen boys: who are no doubt his wife and children. On the walls are reproductions of Constables (one being the 'Hay Wain') in large heavy frames which, in Theo's opinion, do the paintings no favours.

Stephen has some family resemblance to Hannah; he is solidly built, of average height, though he looks less trim than his sister, more jowly. He is dressed in an unflattering suit and his hair is mousy and thinning. Nor does he have her remarkable greeny-hazel eyes; his are rather dull, unremarkable blue behind unimaginative glasses. Suze has informed Theo that Stephen Poole has aspirations to be a magistrate. *How does she know these things?* And he appears to be practising his look-to-intimidate-petty-criminals-with on them. Harry shifts uneasily by Theo's side; she's been more silent than ever today, though has assured him that she's fine. Poole dispenses with any apology, niceties or offers of refreshments, and asks them briskly what they want. He doesn't have to articulate that he is a very busy man and they are an irritant; this is implicit in his tone and manner. Theo forces himself to smile and amuses himself by giving a rather long and leisurely explanation. Stephen looks cross, says he did at one time give Dr Greene some financial advice, but he had by no means been her adviser and has no knowledge of her current financial situation. They had had no contact for some years and couldn't Theo have ascertained this over the phone? Theo continues to smile. Perhaps Mr Poole would be so good as to outline the nature of his advice and Dr Greene's situation at that time? Stephen sighs. 'Alright, we're talking ten, eleven years ago, so don't expect me to be accurate.' He sits back in his leather chair. It creaks gently. 'Dr Greene was keen to get rid of the Centre and leave the town. I believe there was a domestic issue, I got the impression it was complicated. One of my other clients gave her my name and she rang me up. We had a bit of a chat, I suggested some ways she might manage the transfer of the business without incurring unnecessary taxes on a sale and that was it.'

'And you haven't spoken to her since?'

'No.'

Sun floods the room, only the fresh spring air is kept at bay by triple glazing. Theo thinks maybe he and Harry will have a picnic under those blossom trees before making the long drive back, salvage something from the day.

'And none of your dealings since have included Dr Greene?' This from DC Shilling.

A hesitation. Theo wakes himself up again: *Good woman, Harry.* Finally Poole says, less sure of himself now, 'Dr Greene loaned Max Harris some money to help him with his business. I understand they met because Max's wife knew the girl who was, er, involved with Dr Greene at the time. I offered advice on how to negotiate and contract for the loan.' Another pause, then: 'Max has been in touch recently to say he's due to repay the loan and he can't afford to but Dr Greene is, was, insisting, so he needed to know where best to get the money to pay his debt off.'

'And get into more debt?' Theo says, more a statement than a question.

Stephen gives a half-shrug, half-nod. 'It's not unusual these days to take out a loan to pay back a loan. Usually it's for credit-card debt and to get a more manageable rate of interest.'

'Was Mr Harris paying interest to Dr Greene?' asks Harry.

'No. It was an interest-free loan.'

'That was generous of Dr Greene,' says Theo.

'As I said, she was looking for investments to ease her tax burden.'

Harry comes in again with her gentle, almost casual tone. 'So Mr Harris has gone from having an interest-free loan to having to find interest every month?'

'I don't believe the transaction was completed.'

'And now Dr Greene's dead?'

Poole's shoulders express his impatience to be done. 'He still owes the inheritor of the estate, who I'm guessing is the, er, civil partner, so it would be down to Penny Greene whether she insists on calling it in or renegotiates a continuance. I imagine that wouldn't be top of her priority list; however, I could be wrong.'

Theo has a sudden thought. 'Did Max meet with Dr Greene? I mean when Dr Greene came back to Scarborough for her last flying visit, before she was killed.'

'I understood from Max that that was his intention. He thought face to face he could persuade Dr Greene to change her mind.'

'And the meeting took place when?'

Stephen Poole lifts his chubby hands. 'I don't know if it did take place, I haven't spoken to Max since the phone call when he told me all this. I believe it was scheduled for the 22nd of February.'

The day Dr Greene had her head smashed in with a hammer. None of them need to say it: it is writ large in the turgid air. Theo wants to get out and breathe again. He has played football with Max, shared a pint, he's big, he's a bit crude at times and can be quick to temper, enough to be a killer? Theo doesn't like his criminals quite so closely associated with him, a hazard of working in a small town.

The welcome lacked charm and the parting is equally perfunctory. Once outside Theo suggests his picnic idea to Harry and she declines, saying she wants to get back before the traffic builds up. As she is driving, he feels he can hardly overrule her, though he wonders how she would manage in a metropolis where Scarborough's idea of a rush hour would be laughed at. He notices how tired she is looking. It can't be this case: after the first flurry of activity, he's not been allowed to permit overtime. Poor Harry. Theo wants to give her a big hug and tell her whatever is troubling her will pass. Instead he buys them both ice creams on the way back to the car.

Chapter 19

Max jiggles from one foot to the other, the baby in his arms. He is talking about her going back to work; she'd said she would want to. (*Did I?* Aurora strains to remember herself in the pre-Oliver days.) And his sister and mum could babysit where necessary, Max continues. (Aurora recalls getting on with these two plump, enthusiastically maternal women in another universe. Now they seem as threatening as rival mother bears.) They could do with the money. *(Could they? Has something happened to his business that he's not telling her?)* She is crying (again). She lifts her feet onto the runners and the chair rocks gently. She stares out at the weeping garden. Tiredness drifts through her like a miasma. He comes between her and the window, looming above her. His head is larger, more oblong than it used to be, she's sure, fusing into his neck. It occurs to her that this might not be Max. Would her husband be so insistent she leave his offspring with others? In this the imposter has got it wrong and has given himself away. She continues to rock, faster, then faster again. She must be cautious. *If this isn't Max, then perhaps this isn't my house either. I've been kidnapped and imprisoned somewhere.* Her jailors having gone to exceptional lengths to make her surroundings look familiar to her.

'Aurora, for goodness sake, stop that, you're going to damage the paintwork.'
The Max lookalike puts out his large hand. She now clearly sees in the rain-stained glass, it is a hair-covered paw. He steadies her chair as it is banging against the wall. *One more proof that I'm not in my own home: even the walls are in the wrong place.* His smell is so similar to Max's, like a fresh breeze on an early spring morning, that she nearly forgets and tells him she's a hostage. She so wants to tell someone, she could almost believe it is him, just because she wants to. A rhythmic screech starts up in her brain, now they are trying to force their way in there too, she imagines a dentist's drill whirring away at her temple. No, it is a call for him, from one of his handlers.

The baby is on her lap, the baby the Max-fraudster calls Oliver; though, of course, it isn't. She would know her own baby, wouldn't she? She hasn't had hers yet, it is still dormant inside her. She wraps her arms protectively around herself, looks down at the baby balanced there on her knees. Perhaps he's not even a real child, all that mass of black hair, those darkening eyes, those claws which are grasping at air. She understands now, he's a little wolf cub. Listen as he howls.

'Aurora, I can't hear myself speak,' the Max-who-is-not shouts. He apologises down the phone to someone called Fiona. *(Who is she? His other, his real, wife?)* Then turns back to Aurora: 'Pick him up or something.'

Watch as the mouth grows into a snout filled with gleaming, pointing teeth.

'Aurora!'

He'll snap, he'll bite, he'll scratch, because he knows, he knows, you are not his mother, you're his prey. She flings herself backwards out of the way of those voracious jaws.

'Jesus, Aurora, be careful, you'll drop—. Shit! Fiona, I'll call you back.'

The baby's shrieking becomes so loud that she has to cover her ears, only she can't block out the shouting.

'What the hell were you doing? Why weren't you holding on to him? Oliver, are you OK? Let me have a look. Shh, it's OK, it's OK, Daddy's here, you're OK, you're OK, hush now, hush now.'

She looks round. Max has Oliver hugged to him, he's gently moving backwards and forwards, patting the child's back, murmuring in his ear and slowly, slowly the crying diminishes. She stands up. 'What happened? What happened to him?'

Max opens his eyes. His face is the colour of squashed raspberries. 'What happened?' he explodes, then repeats it more softly as Oliver whimpers. 'How can you ask that, Aurora? You let him fall. Hell, you dropped him. What were you thinking of?'

She shakes her head, meaning to negate what he is saying; she strangles a sob. 'Is he hurt?' She brushes her fingers against the soft wool of Oliver's cardigan.

'As if you care,' retorts Max. He pulls Oliver away from his shoulder to examine his face.

Aurora sees the little pink mark appearing on the baby's milky-brown skin above the thin dark line of his eyebrow. 'No,' she breathes.

'See what you've done? You've really hurt him, you idiot. This could have been serious, Aurora, you could have done a hell of a lot of damage. What the bloody hell were you thinking of?' His raised voice starts Oliver off again, only it is as if he is all out of tears and he gulps up liquid from the pit of his stomach onto Max's front. 'Jesus Christ. This is all your doing, Aurora. Come on, Oliver, we'll go and get ourselves cleaned up.' He turns to go, shouting as he goes out of the room, 'You're not fit to be a fucking mother, Aurora!'

The smell of sick makes Aurora gag, the acid corrodes the back of her throat. At Max's final blast, she stumbles and ends up crouched on the floor, her back against the wall. She keeps one hand clamped firmly across her mouth, the other cradling her abdomen. He's wrong, so wrong: she would make a good mother. But she sees now the danger she is in. If he tells them, reports back to them, then they will take her baby away, the one who is at this moment sleeping peacefully beneath the hollow of her palm.

Aurora now sees how careful she has to be, to keep intact the façade she is hiding behind. She understands the consequences of letting go of everything, of letting it all slip. Her Max has already been replaced, this strange changeling has been put in her care. It is a test, there is no other explanation. She has to concentrate, to adapt, she's always been good at that, it got her through school, through examinations; and in concentrating she begins to comprehend things with a greater clarity.

Survival is her first instinct. Submit and survive. At this moment it seems the only option. If she gives away what she knows, then they would have no choice but to get rid of her. On the other hand, if she goes along with it for now, perhaps she can learn enough to plan her escape, to find out what they have done with her husband, though she suspects he is way past her help by now. No, she is on her own, thrown back on her own resources. She will watch, listen and wait for her opportunity.

She does think that she might get in touch with her parents. Perhaps she could write, as she does not trust the phone or the internet. She could explain everything to them, ask them to come and rescue her. How glad she is that she did not do that, for she has received the warning message. How could she have been so dim as not to see them before? For they are everywhere, clues left for her, communications from a mysterious protector. She must take account of them. The creature in the cot by her side mews gently to himself, catches his hind claws in his front ones, he draws back his too-red lips. She has seen the augury she's been waiting for on the page of the book in front of her. The small girl enters the little wooden cabin in the woods to bring the food and drink to her granny. Only something is wrong. Aurora had previously thought the story was that the wolf was pretending to be the granny, now she realises she was mistaken. It isn't like that at all. The granny, the child's closest and dearest relation, has become a wild carnivorous animal.

The wolf pup loves to be outside. Aurora puts him in the pram and immediately he quietens, becomes attentive, watchful. As they start down the cliff path he reaches and flexes his fingers towards the miniature white celandine flowers that congregate amongst the grass. Aurora picks one for him and for a moment he is able to hold it, lifting it to his nose until his coordination deserts him and he drops it. He is unconcerned by this loss, his interest taken by the movement of the pink-edged leaves of the hebes, ruffled by the hyacinth-scented breeze, and then by a red admiral butterfly. They walk on; he occasionally quietly chuntering to himself, Aurora silent. She notices the plastic bags and cans abandoned amongst the fecund vegetation and thinks

113

sourly of her own species. They meet two specimens, the man unkempt in clothes which were meant to fit someone smaller, the woman needle-thin apart from her egg-white distended belly protruding between T-shirt and trackie bottoms. Aurora and Oliver are ignored; the couple's vacant eyes are preoccupied with their goal: one of the Victorian shelters that dot the slopes, where they can consume their booty. Later Aurora will see them hurling monosyllabic insults at each other by the straggling roses of the cliff gardens; now, however, there is a conspiratorial intimacy which keeps them scuttling along together.

Aurora and Oliver (finally sleeping) come to rest by the concrete wall that rises from the beach. The wind is chillier here, speaking of oceanic journeys, and the sea is scuffling against its margins as if there is not enough room for all that it carries. Clouds skid across the sun and sky and patch the flat, steely water. Seating herself by some steps which would normally go down to sand but at present disappear into the lolling waves, Aurora finds a refuge from the cold blast and a little peace. The liquid world is scornful of those who are land-bound: it knows about infinity, about how smallest particles can add up to greatness when moving as one, about what's hidden in the depths. Aurora stares and stares, hoping to learn something of this. Only she is a mere creature tethered to soil and the sea won't give up her secrets to her. Aurora turns away, her eyes stinging.

She's brought the local paper with her, the only reading matter she's had the capacity to digest for many weeks. For no good reason that she can see, certainly not for its newsworthiness, the paper has regurgitated the details of Dr Themis Greene's death onto its front page. The main point to the story appears to be the lack of progress in finding the killer. Aurora stops for a few moments over the date of the murder: there's something about it which snags at her brain, though she can't quite bring it out of the fug. She gives up and leafs on through. There's someone who has written a book about local witches. About Hannah Leigh, who walked the cliff paths at midnight collecting her ingredients — sorrel, saxifrage, Herb-Robert, perhaps a rodent or a snake or a bat. And sometimes, it was said, she would sing and fish would leap right out of the sea, flying up the steep incline and into her waiting lap. Footsteps come to a halt by Aurora's side and someone greets her. She looks up and knows the wild-haired woman wrapped in a dark, heavy wool cape to be called Hannah, maybe Hannah Leigh. 'You know this to be where the witches walk?'

Hannah tilts her head on one side like a gull's; after a while she says, 'Is that right?' She sits down beside Aurora and enfolds her in half of her cape so that the two women are sharing it. 'Well, they chose a chilly spot for it, didn't they?'

Aurora sees the spark of green in Hannah's eyes and that her skin is woven from the ivory light of the new moon. Aurora feels shriven, she feels blessed.

****

Stan Poole has argued with his daughter because she has told him she won't be voting in the local elections in a few weeks' time. He is now on the phone arguing with his son because he intends to vote Conservative and Stan Poole considers this an insult to his (increasingly dubious, to Hannah's mind) claim to being working class. It is the febrile atmosphere in the house that sends her out into the cooler air. She now sees how often her father choreographs these disagreements to express the disappointments he feels (in his children, in his life, perhaps even in himself) yet cannot properly articulate. Her feet pound his anger and her own into the pavement. As she realises this she eases up on herself and on the pace. According to Lawrence (who is apparently allowed to employ his blue vote with impunity) Stan is in for further disappointments, the routing of Labour in the coming polls and then in the general election next year, which Brown will try to defer as long as he can. There had been no heat in his exposition; Lawrence was more interested in telling her about Theo. *What, Detective Sergeant Theo Akande?*

115

Hannah could tell Lawrence is smitten. She is happy for him, disconcerted for herself. Might this be the policeman's ploy to reignite his stalled investigation? Not that Lawrence would say anything to arouse suspicions about her; he knows nothing of her guilt, transferred into her, like a flake of skin conveyed in a handshake. She tries to walk herself out of herself, willing the wind to pick the guilt from her as it might carry off the brittle autumn leaves from trees which have no more use for them. When she could steer Lawrence away from talking about Theo, she asked what he thought of Ben. He hadn't changed much; witty, yes, but just that little bit too earnest, and still overly fascinated by the minutiae of his interests, like facts on obscure music bands or unknown comedy programmes. Pretending to herself that she didn't care what the response would be, Hannah had asked whether he'd said anything about his girlfriend. 'What girlfriend? Ben doesn't have a girlfriend,' Lawrence had replied. Adding: 'Too self-absorbed, most likely.'

By the time she comes to the shore and sees Aurora, the wind is tugging Hannah's hair every which way and the freeze is beginning to penetrate into her marrow. She had grabbed the first thing that came to hand as she exited the house and it is some old woollen shawl inadequate for keeping out the elements. She doesn't even know who it belongs to. She doubts it's something her mother would have; perhaps it had been forgotten after one of her bridge parties. Hannah spies Aurora hunkered down by the sea wall, the pram parked a little to one side, angled so that the occupant would be open to the icy squall. Hannah starts to make her escape up one of the cliff paths which would allow her to circumvent the mother and baby. She stops and looks back, walks on, hesitates and finally turns around.

She immediately regrets her decision when Aurora greets her with, 'You know this to be where the witches walk?' How is she supposed to respond to that? Hannah notices that Aurora's once gorgeous curves are fast becoming ungainly flab spilling out of her sweatshirt and elasticated trousers, her face is pouched by lack of sleep, her hair is harshly pulled back into a greasy ponytail. Hannah feels a stab of disgust, is going to leave, then sees the other woman shiver, tears in her still-lovely eyes. Hannah grasps around for some appropriate words, then seats herself and pulls her shawl around them both. The smell of seaweed mingles with that of Aurora's now-cooled sweat. Hannah has been reading about depression. There were footnotes on post-natal depression, references to something else ... she searches for the term ... puerperal psychosis? Was it that? Whatever the diagnosis, she knows she is sitting next to one unhappy woman and she has an impulse to hug her, to tell her things will get better. Instead she gives those reddened swollen hands a squeeze. Unnerved by their total absence of warmth, she suggests they go home. There is some mewling from the pram and she adds that she thinks Oliver may need to be fed.

'Oliver?'

'Your baby. In the pram.'

Aurora doesn't move.

'Come on, Aurora, think it's best we get going or we're all going to get hypothermia.' She's praying that Oliver is well covered and/or made of very stern stuff, poor kid.

'I'm scared.'

Hannah stops in her preparations to stand up and to bodily take the other woman with her if necessary. 'What of?'

'Max.'

'He would never hurt you, nor Oliver.' *How do I know?* But the main thing is to get them indoors, everything else can wait until then.

'I used to think that, only I'm not sure any more, I don't know what he's capable of now. He's different, a different person.'

'I guess having a baby changes you. He won't be different underneath.'

'He's more short-tempered, violent.'

'Lack of sleep?' Hannah offers, feeling the lameness of it. 'Come on, Aurora, let's get you home and then we can sort it.'

She turns her large brown eyes, the whites veined red, onto Hannah. 'You'll help me? You won't leave me?'

Hannah can hear Oliver working himself up into a distressingly painful tantrum, so she readily agrees. At last she is able to get Aurora on her feet and is able to lead her homewards while she pushes the pram. Hannah tucks her shawl around the baby, who quietens as they make their slow progress though his skin looks unhealthily sallow. She mutters some reassurances, whether for him or for herself. She says to Aurora that she can only imagine how hard it must be to adjust to becoming a mum, feel responsible for another human being and be without sleep, that maybe seeking some support or advice might be a good thing. Hannah fears her words sound hollow. *What do I know about any of this? Zero.* In any case it doesn't appear that she is being listened to. She only gets a reaction, a kind of sighed 'yes' when she finishes with the inadequate: 'When I was young I would always tell myself stories to get myself off to sleep.'

Finally, they are on the top of the cliff (Hannah having had to persuade Aurora not to approach two druggies arguing in the neglected rose gardens) and they are walking along the Esplanade. Hannah is ten minutes away from being able to hand over her burdens. Then Aurora stops. 'Eve,' she says, and repeats the name with increasing volume. The woman this is directed to is about to go into one of the tall Victorian buildings which contain a number of bay-windowed and balconied flats. It is Dr Greene's partner, Penny. Hannah tries to tell Aurora so, but she rushes up the path and seizes the woman by her bony shoulder. She responds by protesting that she is Penny, over and over, in a voice which is higher pitched than Hannah remembers from the commemoration. However, why wouldn't it be? The woman is quite frankly terrified. She finally gains entrance into the building and slams the heavy door shut behind her. Aurora is left on the doorstep yelling: 'I know you, Eve, why won't you speak to me?'

Whether it is hearing his mother or his own discomfort, Oliver starts to scream. Hannah is on the point of abandoning them both to it. It is the baby's cries twisting something deep down inside which is making her want to run away. She barks at Aurora to come along and the edge in her voice brings the desired result: they are able to set off again at speed and Hannah doesn't let up until they have reached her neighbour's front door. It is a huge relief to find Max waiting for them. He rounds angrily on his wife, roughly dragging her inside while taking up his child with greater tenderness. He hardly notices Hannah, the pram is discarded outside and the door closed with force. She can hear the cacophony being produced by Max and Oliver going on inside the house; there is no sound from Aurora. Hannah wonders whether she should do something, knock, insist she be allowed to enter, intervene. Then a howl from the baby drives staples into her intestines and she quickly backs away.

Chapter 20

I am not a bad person; I don't … I don't … I don't murder people … do I? For a moment she is in another therapy room watching herself smash Dr Greene's skull open with a hammer. With a struggle, she banishes the image. *I am not a bad person.* These are the words waiting to be said. Yet Hannah knows deep down that she is bad, she was born bad, somehow. She has to make strenuous efforts to cover this up — both the knowledge and the actuality of it. Under Izzie's kind — though nevertheless assessing — gaze, Hannah is running out of the energy she needs to keep up the pretence. Izzie does not look away, unlike most people. Most people see the seam of badness barely camouflaged by smiles and — Hannah likes to think — a certain endearing quirkiness, and they turn away. They are afraid. Izzie is not afraid. This realisation terrifies Hannah. She is a dung beetle caught and pinned to an observation board, her legs waggling uselessly in the air in their efforts to carry her away from the light. From Izzie's microscopic vision. Izzie will see through the incongruent, filched incandescent dragonfly wings; she will poke into the dull armour casing; and she will discover what's underneath.

Increasingly the sessions come to this point, however carefully Hannah prepares. This time she had constructed a story around what — in her view — was a quite remarkable flash of genius: what had happened between Clarke, James and her was a drama triangle. James was the victim (as ever), she was the persecutor and Clarke the rescuer (turned persecutor of her). When she had pointed this out to the group she expected some approval, perhaps even some sympathy for her being unwittingly drawn into James's nasty little process. She looked for this particularly from Clarke; he remained cool, asking, nay demanding, 'So what?' *Don't you see?* she wanted to respond. *Don't you see? I'm not to blame. You can love me again.* She didn't say it and even she could feel his disdain for her, probably fuelled, she thought, by her essay being returned with an 'excellent' and his not even being written yet.

120

Then things had gone hideous, with Fred asking her how come she'd stepped into the persecutor role. She'd spat back that she hadn't stepped into it, that was the whole point of drama triangles, she was unwillingly induced, she couldn't help it. 'Is that so?' Fred's florid, chubby chin rested on his steepled fingers, his blue eyes were magnified by his glasses. She'd replied that if he was so clever why hadn't he known what was going on and intervened? 'I did know. And you didn't ask me,' Fred said flatly. A heavy metal lid clanged shut over her head. They were just lab mice to him, losing their way in a maze, scrapping, burrowing uselessly into hard plastic — and all for his amusement. She hated him then. She held herself away from him until her shoulder ached.

Her shoulder is aching now. A pneumatic drill is being driven through it into her brain, pounding home the words: *You chose to be the persecutor because you are a bad, bad person.* From her reading she knows this is not a correct interpretation of the theory, being the persecutor is about her not owning her power, yet she can't make this stick. The drill is too insistent, too overwhelming.

It almost swamps Izzie's enquiry, 'I notice you're sitting quite stiffly, Hannah. What's going on for you right now?'

There's not enough space in her mouth for all the words required to adequately answer this question. There's not enough space in the room for everything that needs to be said. The angry words would sizzle through the air, burning out the oxygen, suffocating them. The sad words would submerge them in tears, drowning them. Either way, the two of them would perish. 'I'm fine.' Hannah tries to inject some bounce but the phrase remains leaden.

No reaction. Izzie is waiting for something other. Eventually she says, 'Talk a bit more, it doesn't matter if it's a jumble.'

A jumble doesn't even begin to render it. Where to start? There's nowhere to start. Or the start is so far back in the past she cannot grasp it. Despair grips drily at her throat and pricks at the tender corners of her eyes. She has reached this point in previous sessions and the futility of continuing the therapy is once again around. *Perhaps I should start seeing someone else, someone who doesn't put me in this corner on such a regular basis. Someone I could talk about other things to, less difficult things. Avoidance? Running away? Or maybe I don't need to do this now. Or ever. After all, I may decide not to be a counsellor.* She looks at Izzie. The other woman is seated back in the squashy black cushions of the sofa opposite. The platinum is more obvious in amongst the short wheat hair. Izzie has tanned slightly in the recent sunny weather *(or maybe she's been away?)* and is wearing a white blouse which shows it off well, with a pair of cut-off trousers instead of the usual jeans. Chips of a purple gemstone — perhaps an amethyst — are patterned into a silver anklet and a matching toe ring. There are fine lines around her small eyes and a faint scar which draws on her thin lips; apart from that her skin is smooth. There have been times when that face has expressed confusion or sadness, possibly even a little irritation. Hannah wonders how deeply it all goes.

'Is there something you want to ask me, Hannah?'

Hannah shakes her head. She doesn't want to know, she merely wants to believe, to believe that Izzie feels something genuine for her.

'I'm thinking it can't have been easy for you to have Clarke being hard on you and then being cold?'

Hannah is taken by surprise at the length of Izzie's sentence. Izzie sometimes does this, eschewing being quiet for once; conceivably she gets fed up waiting. Hannah shrugs.

'Have you tried to talk to him about it?'

The memory of those texts burns through to her face, branding it. Obsessive and manic, two words which fall into the 'disorder' sections of therapy books. She looks down at her fingernails scratching at her knuckles.

'What happened?'

Hannah mutters that she was stupid, an idiot.

'Try to say, "I was feeling vulnerable" instead of berating yourself. Can you describe more about what happened?'

She manages to stumble out some kind of explanation. Though her exterior is ablaze, she feels cold and small inside.

'What were you afraid of, Hannah?' Izzie's voice is incredibly soft.

'Of being alone.' It comes out as a startlingly strangled cry.

'And when were you most alone?'

She shakes her head.

'What does it feel like?'

'Cold, I'm very cold and no-one is coming to get me, to help me. I don't want to be here any more.' Her distress crashes over her, the chilly waves of the North Sea bashing into her chest. She can hardly breathe.

'Breathe, Hannah, and tell me what's happening for you.'

'It's my own fault, it's my punishment.'

'For what?'

Hannah looks up. The round face has moved forward, a notch has appeared between eyes which have darkened, are offering something. Salvation? Maybe. She says it very quietly, then repeats it, stuttering, 'I'm evil.'

'Are you?' Izzie sounds startled, not shocked. She does not turn away. 'What have you done?'

Hannah continues in a whisper: she doesn't know, she simply is, born that way, she has to work hard to keep it in check.

'Or what?'

Hannah can't answer this. She reiterates what she has just said, knowing that she is repeating herself and not knowing what else to say. She trails to a stop, her stomach contracted, anticipating the inevitable blow.

Izzie takes a moment before saying, 'I understand that's how you feel, Hannah, and I really appreciate you telling me that's how you feel. And I want you to hear that I see no evidence that you are evil. I do not experience you that way.'

'You must.'

'I don't.' She's smiling.

'You're lying.'

'I'm not.'

'Then ... then ...' Hannah's head is swarming with mosquitoes, their wings and proboscis snapping into the delicate neurones until they start fizzing. 'Then you're stupid!' She looks at Izzie's face and lets it go out of focus: she can't bear to see it turn to anger. She hears Izzie telling her to leave and begins to pull on her jacket.

'Are you going, Hannah? We've ten minutes left, I think.'

Hannah is on her feet, saying she can't stay.

'What's stopping you staying?'

'You hate me.' Hannah halts, staring at her feet in their strappy red sandals on the dark carpet. Things inside her head and outside are at least quiet. Izzie urges her to sit again and reluctantly she does so. After more encouragement she allows herself an askance view of the other woman and finds that she is being smiled at.

'I don't hate you. I must admit my pride is a little sore that you should consider me stupid, though I know I can be at times. Right now you need me to reject you to fortify this belief that you hold that you are evil. I won't do that. However, I do understand that you believe at a very deep level that you are evil. It's an important step that you have shared this with me. I want to thank you for doing that. I want you to come back next week and I think you will find it hard to do, so is there something I can say or do which will help you to accept I don't hate you and want you here?'

At that moment, Hannah wants to be hugged, wants to be held, held together, so her sides aren't wrenched apart. But it would feel too wonderful, to have that comfort, so she does not allow it and she shakes her head.

Izzie withdraws her open hands into her lap, where they embrace each other. 'You're a writer, aren't you?'

Hannah is tugged into the present by the surprise question. 'I edit and proofread other people's writing,' she says hesitantly.

'But you write well yourself. You've had good marks for your essays and didn't you say you'd put some poetry in one?'

'I wouldn't call it poetry.'

Izzie, for once, appears tentative. 'I've been thinking recently: maybe you could write, write your story, when you can't speak it.'

She isn't interested; on the other hand Izzie has just admitted thinking about her outside of sessions. She wants to luxuriate in that a little. 'How do you mean?'

'Keep a journal, write in it every day for about fifteen minutes, whatever comes; and then, if you want, share some of it here, with me.'

'I could give it a try, I suppose.' *If I do this, Izzie won't throw me out.*

'Good.' She smiles broadly. 'You are fine, Hannah, just as you are. Try to hold on to that this week.'

Hannah nods, already rejecting it, then pulls out her purse and her diary.

Chapter 21

There are instances when Hannah begins to see beyond the exterior. Past the just-too-cheap shiny light-grey suits; the comic or over-bright ties; the over-coiffured, over-dark hair; the patronising 'darling's and 'love's; and into a deeper someone. She is starting to glimpse below the crust of Darren Frost, to a person desperately trying too hard to be a somebody. And though she finds it hard to feel any affection for her client, she can at least feel affinity for the desperation and the endeavour.

'I wasn't like that until she came along,' he says.

Hannah swallows back down her immediate response of 'pillock', knowing her desire to 'wipe him out' (as Orwell puts it) is a replaying from something deep in his childhood. She attempts instead to weed back through the long and involved tale he is telling her and extract an essential meaning. 'It's not my fault,' suddenly screams out at her. She remembers the scraps of Darren's biography which she has managed to glean. The idolised father who left the family before his son was three, apparently chased out by his wife. Then there was the appearance of a stepfather who, though caring (as far as Hannah can work out), was never good enough (a sense Hannah shares with this oh-so-ordinary man when she sits in the company of Darren Frost week after week). Darren has paused for a moment, maybe waiting for some kind of approbation of his version of events. Hannah has lost track of exactly where he is in explaining why his most recent relationship hasn't worked out. He is rubbing his hands together, as he often does, a kind of getting-rid gesture. His narrowed eyes are as non-reflective as oil.

Hannah says gently, 'It wasn't your fault, Darren.'

He nods and says (as he frequently does) that whoever it is he's been talking about should be sitting here not him.

'No, I mean,' she has to raise her voice slightly, 'it wasn't your fault that your dad left.'

He hesitates for a fraction before continuing with his treatise on the unstableness of womankind.

'Darren, did you hear what I said?' He is not listening, or at least pretending not to, though she can see the tension fixing his fidgeting fingers, paralysing him slowly up through his arms and into his face until his features have become a mask. 'Darren, stop,' she says loudly. To her surprise he does and she repeats that it is not his fault his father left, though now the certainty that this is the correct thing to be saying is draining away.

He laughs stiffly. 'I know. It was my mum, she sent him away.'

She crashes in: 'You may know that in your head, Darren, but you don't feel it, do you?'

'Feelings: you therapists are always going on about feelings, thinking now that's what's important for a man; feelings are—.'

'No, Darren, right now it is your feelings that are important and you feel to blame for your dad leaving. And you weren't to blame.' Hannah is gripping on to her belief that this is the right way to go; she remembers Orwell's encouragement to 'trust your gut. You've got a handy gut sense, Hannah.' She focuses on the mask and those oil sumps in front of her. She wants to drag them out the way, reveal what's underneath; involuntarily she sits forward. She allows the silence to descend between them. Darren drops his gaze, a nerve in his cheek twitches. He starts off on his womankind-are-from-hell theory again. Hannah interrupts. 'You are not to blame that he left.' This non-exchange happens for a second, then a third time. Hannah holds her ground.

'So? So? You say I wasn't to blame, so what?' Darren tosses at her angrily, sharply raising his head. His eyes are fast melting, he rubs at them harshly. He carries on, his voice grating, 'He still went, didn't he?'

'He did go. And it wasn't your fault.'

Darren covers a sob with a cough. 'I'm not going to cry,' he shouts. 'That's what you want, isn't it, you therapists? That I cry? Well, I'm not going to.'

Hannah offers him a box of tissues which he rejects taking out his purple handkerchief from his chest pocket and blowing his nose on it. She notices the time: the hour has galloped to its conclusion; for the first time with Darren she would like it to go on longer. However, Orwell's strictures pull her upright, plus she has only thirty minutes before Elsa comes in. She has a momentary panic: how does she conclude? How can she eject him when he's obviously distressed? She notices that finally she feels some warmth towards the man sitting in front of her. 'Our time together is nearly up.'

'Yes, that's right,' Darren fumes. 'Now you've got me in this state throw me out, just like all the others.'

Hannah gulps. She wants to rush in with all sorts of reassurances; once again guidance from Fred and Orwell comes to mind. 'And I will be here for you next week, Darren. We can talk further then.'

'And I suppose I have to pay you for this too.'

'That's the deal.'

He pulls out his wallet and throws two tenners in her direction. They float to the floor.

'Thank you, Darren. I will see you next week.'

'Maybe, or maybe I'll find another therapist, get a second opinion, as they say.' His voice no longer expresses his fury: it is cold, his face and his eyes frozen. 'Goodbye.' He leaves, closing the door gently behind him, though Hannah feels it slammed in her face. She whimpers. She shivers. She slumps down into the chair, becoming conscious of the stiffness that had invaded her own body. For a moment she thinks, *That's it, I can't do this any more, I'm so fucking useless, stupid.* Then hears Orwell enjoining her to say 'interesting' rather than 'stupid'. She tells her supervisor to shut up, but nevertheless rouses herself enough to write up some notes and in doing so realises that just maybe something useful has come out of the session.

Refreshed by a brief walk in the Centre's front yard, cadging some breaths of warm, early-summer air, and a quick cup of coffee, Hannah is feeling quite ebullient when Elsa arrives.

128

In contrast with Darren, Hannah looks forwards to her sessions with Elsa, who chose to come and see her privately after her six-week GP-referred stint was up. Elsa's headaches have gone, her back has eased and Dr Courtney, Hannah suspects, is only too glad to see less of her contrary patient. Hannah sometimes worries that her sessions with Elsa are too cosy, too conversational, they are too much like teenage siblings enjoying an illicit midnight feast. Elsa is a fairground ride, sometimes shooting up in the air, sometimes dipping into shadowed tunnels, then out again, before Hannah has time to catch her breath. She can tell from what Elsa is wearing where the session is going to start off; today the younger woman is wearing a skirt and top striped in yellow and red which don't quite match, her hair is teased into a blonde frizzy topknot and she has on an enormous pair of polka-dotted plastic earrings. And they have barely sat down before she is off on her story about her latest love, the one who is far better than any she has had before. Her mother hates him, so that must be a good sign. She laughs and describes how they met by accident when he'd been in Scarborough for the weekend and had asked her the way to the beach. They'd been inseparable for forty-eight hours and hadn't stopped phoning and texting since he went back to Manchester, where he's staying.

'Staying?'

'Looking for a job. If he doesn't find one soon he might have to go back home.'

'Home?'

Elsa hesitates for a fraction. 'Poland?' she says uncertainly. 'Or the Ukraine, maybe.'

'He speaks good English, then.'

'I can learn his language, I was good at languages at school.' She's beginning to sound sulky.

'You'd better find out what it is, in that case.'

'We speak the language of lu-urve, anyway,' Elsa responds, lifting her chin a fraction. 'Whatever happens, I know we'll be together.'

Hannah suppresses her desire to point out to Elsa how ridiculous this is (too much like Elsa's mother). She also holds off on any more questions: slow her down, Orwell has advised, let a breathing space come in.

Elsa isn't keen on hush. She gallops into her next tale, about her job: she's found another one and she's very happy, everyone is so nice to her. Somewhere in the middle of all this she talks about applying for a job with a local design firm but realising at the interview she'd slept with the owner. 'I don't think he recognised me. Not with all my clothes on.' Again she laughs. It's infectious. Hannah smiles, though she doesn't want to. She is momentarily troubled by Max's name coming to her mind. She doesn't ask who the prospective employer was. She doesn't want to know more. Focus on Elsa. When she does so, Hannah notices how juvenile Elsa appears today, despite being nearly thirty, only a few years younger than Hannah. Hannah continues to concentrate on the lively gestures of the woman sitting opposite, letting the chatter wash around her, an incoming tide. Then Elsa halts. 'You're looking very stern. You think I'm going to make an idiot of myself again, don't you?'

Hannah pauses before speaking, her only opportunity to bring quiet into the room; then she says slowly, 'I'm feeling very protective of you, Elsa. I don't want you to get hurt. I feel sad too. You're obviously very up today, full of energy, and that's wonderful to experience with you. I just wonder if there's anything else going on for you?'

A shadow creeps across the blandly painted walls; maybe a cloud has edged over the sun for a moment. Elsa's shoulders droop, she lets out a sigh. 'Of course, I'm worried that things won't work out, that I'll scare him off by wanting him too much, you know, like we talked about.' She looks up. Her hands could be in an attitude of prayer, 'He is gorgeous, Hannah, you should see him, I've a photo on my phone, it's not very good, should I show it?' She shakes her head. 'No, no, I remember, no phones in here. Anyway, I'm afraid to look.'

130

Everything has finally slowed and their voices are both hushed. 'What are you afraid of?'

'He hasn't — he hasn't texted me since last night.' Pause for a moment; her face looks doughy and unbaked. 'I've done it again, haven't I, Hannah? I've scared him off. Mum will be ecstatic to be able to say I told you so. Again.'

Ah, the treachery of the text. For a second Hannah remembers her own barraging of Clarke and wants to shrink into herself. With an effort, she pushes that to one side. 'I don't know, Elsa. I don't know what's stopping him from contacting you. Let's stick with what we know, and that's how you're feeling right now.'

'Empty, empty. It's horrible, Hannah.' Elsa is quick to tears, despite her flamboyance. She cries undemonstratively, accepting the tissues passed over accompanied by a discreet squeeze of the hand. Finally she sits up, her nose pink and her mouth pinched, a younger version of her mum, for whom the pinching has become permanent. 'You think I should finish with him. If he hasn't already finished with me.'

'It's not for me to say what you do, Elsa. You know what your options are.'

'Finish with him. Or not. Carry on as I have been doing or …' she smiles mischievously, 'not. I guess I could back off a little. Text him once a day. Or maybe twice.'

'He might think you are cooling if you don't give him an explanation.'

'I could try and explain, though I'm not sure he'd get it.' A little twist of the mouth. 'He doesn't understand English very well.'

'You can only do what you can do.'

She nods. 'The language of lu-urve doesn't translate very well into text.' And the two of them giggle together, a couple of impish adolescents.

Chapter 22

Aurora hasn't slept. Aurora doesn't sleep. For days, for weeks, it feels like. Oliver sleeps — quite well for a baby if his grandmothers and aunt are to be believed. At first Aurora would sleep. She would fall into a pit of nothingness when Oliver slept or when someone else took over his care. Or she thinks she remembers doing so. Much as she thinks she remembers she was once a solicitor; she was determined to get pregnant and was excited when it happened; she was convinced the birth and the few weeks after would be the lowest point. Now that initiation into motherhood appears positively halcyon.

Aurora prowls with the night creatures. She sits in the dark on the flagged step leading from the French windows into the garden. There is no moon, the stars are spyholes in the blackout cloth dome overhead, telescope lenses turned inwards. A bat flits in loops from eaves to tree bough to gazebo and back again. Something rustles in the hedge: a domestic cat, perhaps, or feral one. There's the stringent scent of something caught and rotting. It's been another hot day. The night is cool and damp. It seeps into Aurora's cotton shift, her slack stomach flesh goosebumps. She glances down at her toes, her chipped nails — *weren't they once manicured?* — have been dipped in blood. A slug is easing itself from grass to step; she watches its ponderous progress.

She has lost her baby. She knows that now. Or perhaps her pregnancy was a false one and she was only ever a surrogate. Either way, she is now custodian to this strange infant from some netherworld. She feels some tenderness towards him, at times, when he is fed and clean and he reaches his chubby fingers towards hers. She lets him hold hers, relishing the warmth of skin on skin, responding to his melodic gabbling. Then there are the other times when his hands grow talons, his gums fangs. His screams screw through her, pinning her liver, her kidneys, her stomach together on a skewer. His body arches away from her. Nothing she does can quieten him. 'What do you want, Oliver? Tell me,' she says desperately. He thumps her arm

132

with his fist. She looks into his eyes, his pupils a camera aperture opened wide. He wants to capture her as their slave, in bondage to those that live beyond the night's fabric.

She looks up at them now and silently asks them why. Why should they want such a useless, stupid and ugly specimen of humankind as herself? She looks back at the slug who is now halfway to her feet and feels an unbearable kinship. She heaves some parched sobs and then tells herself off: 'No good feeling sorry for yourself, Aurora. Pick yourself up and get on with it, that's the only way.'

She gets up, not as quickly or easily as she would have liked, and strides back into the house, absent-mindedly leaving the doors wide open, much to the delight of the slug. She will watch Max finding it the next morning as it has almost reached the crumb-covered top of a kitchen cabinet. Max will take it outside to deluge it in salt.

Aurora is now padding around the dark house. She climbs the stairs. She can hear her husband's lookalike snoring from their bedroom and the child's breathy sighs when she checks in on him. She gets herself a glass of water from the bathroom and considers for a moment the bottle of sleeping pills Dr Courtney prescribed for her. *No, that's what they are waiting for, for me to go to sleep. I mustn't let that happen.* She goes down to the little office on the ground floor and sits at the desk. There is a small pile of papers, some of them bills — wasn't she always responsible for this kind of thing? She searches through the drawers and finds a chequebook which she painstakingly fills in. Later Max will discover it as he files away the bills, which are all paid by direct debit. He will begin to ask her about cheques made out in red to 'Them' and 'Spying sky', he'll give up in front of her blank look, and then will quietly shred them. Aurora also pulls out the desk diary she and Max used to share to ensure they didn't double-book each other or themselves. It has 'his' and 'her' columns; she had added a column for 'Oliver' from March onwards. It is mostly blank. She flips through until she finds some entries. Eventually, she hesitates over a date, the 22nd of February, and the words: '4pm Dr Greene' in the 'his' column. Her mind searches for the significance of this but has to abandon the effort when she hears the familiar start-up wail of Oliver wanting to be fed.

****

Theo hasn't slept. Much. For the previous three weeks his sleeping patterns have been erratic as he headed up the search for a thirteen-year-old girl who had gone missing. He was pretty convinced that she would turn up safe and well. As indeed she did, yesterday, reported on by an alert Youth Hostel member of staff, where she'd been staying with her boyfriend, who is eighteen and had been acquired through Facebook. Still, all the usual procedures for a missing child had had to be gone through and there were moments when Theo started to distrust his instincts and fear that they would find a body in the undergrowth of the near-by woods.

This is the first night since it all started that Theo could have slept a decent stretch. Yet it is 2am and he is seated on a camp chair in the little yard at the back of his rented two-up-two-down terrace, dressed in shorts and T-shirt, a chilled bottle of lager by his side. The air is stuffy in these crowded streets near the centre of town. There's some music seeping from someone's open window, a Bryan Adams track perhaps. Cars occasionally trundle along one of the roads that criss-cross the area. Seagulls pass overhead, dove-grey phantoms in the dark, giving out their guttural cackles. Theo tries to distract himself by identifying some of the constellations. He is not very good: his amateur-astronomer uncle would be disappointed that his patient tutoring had been all but forgotten.

Theo's thoughts continue their disordered race. He is pleased with how he handled the search for the girl, and has received commendation for it from senior staff plus (more importantly) from colleagues. Now, however, there will be the clearing-up of the mess. The fractured familial relationships —

the girl still professing love for the lad — and what to do with him. Scarcely more than a child himself in terms of his maturity, his five years' seniority makes him culpable. A supposed sighting of the runaway in London had given Theo a chance to snatch a hurried lunch with Lawrence. It had not been a success. A previous weekend together had been, though Theo had stayed in the spare room and any touching had been more companionable than anything else. During the lunch Lawrence had been frankly overbearing, as well as uninterested in what Theo was going through. Yet since then, Lawrence's texts and emails have been concerned, verging on the intimate. 'And what do you want, Theo?' That question had come from a conversation with his sister. *I don't want to be played around, I've had enough of that.* Men who won't make a commitment, either because they equate being gay with being unfettered or because they are scared. Theo suspects Lawrence is in the latter camp. *Even so, I don't want to let him go.*

A window is opened across the alley, a child cries, a toilet is flushed. Theo feels hemmed in. Suze has been ribbing him about his unwillingness to look for a home to buy. She's unconvinced by his arguments that he likes the newly renovated house he is in and the rent is very fair. 'Admit it, you're not staying, you're destined for a higher plain,' she said, adding in a dramatic tone, 'Scotland Yard.' He'd joked about the lack of similarity between the Met and Nirvana. Even so, he knows she has a point. He had fully intended to buy (for the first time) when he moved to Scarborough and he hasn't bothered to sign up for any estate-agent details. Maybe he's just more comfortable renting, he consoles himself: buying, being mortgaged, it's a British obsession anyway; across the Channel nobody bothers.

He has today off, he will find a piece of beach to sizzle on, somewhere in amongst the melee, if it's going to be hot, then persuade Ben to meet him for a meal and a film in the evening. He will break himself out of his lassitude. Then it will be back to work and — this has been nagging at him — he will have to question Max about Dr Greene. The DI has been happy to let it all lie while the headlines were all about missing girls, but he doesn't want an unsolved murder lingering any more than Theo does. If Theo can't come up with an alternative, Douglas Olds will have to be questioned again and, in all probability, charged, unless he's changed his story radically.

****

Hannah hasn't slept. At least it doesn't feel like it. In her dreams she is running, running, more than she ever would in her waking world. Or hiding, jamming herself into the smallest spaces — under beds, in cupboards, even in a rabbit hutch — and the person (or people) chasing her with harmful intent remains faceless, nameless, a mystery. She wakes herself, pushing back the dark folds until she can snap her eyes open and see again the accustomed surroundings of her bedroom. Has she called out? Nothing stirs in the house, though a seagull screeches as it skitters down the roof tiles before taking off. Pale cerulean light glimmers around the edges of the blinds covering the Velux windows. The heavy brown-wood dresser with ornate mirror and drawers plus wardrobe, which once belonged to a great-aunt and had been stuck up here out of the way, are sentinel creatures in the shadows. Hannah had disliked them for being old-fashioned and ugly on finding them in the room she was to stay in; now she feels a certain fondness for their familiarity. The desk under one of the windows holds her laptop, some books; though more of those, along with files, are dumped on the floor. Stuck in a holder are a few photos of Lawrence and of herself with Rickie and Steff plus others at various parties, some posher than others. Last night, distracted from an essay, she had looked at herself in her once treasured (second-hand) Versace gown, from his 2002 collection, a figure-hugging peach-coloured affair with acres of chiffon feathering out around her ankles. She had wondered who that young woman was.

    Now she dare not sleep. If she sleeps the terror will close in on her again. Yet she is tired, so tired. She is stiff, her veins shot through with thin metal rods. If she could let some of the tension out, she could sleep. She creeps out of bed, down the stairs. She doesn't need to turn on lights: even at 4:30am there is enough filtering in from the outside. Floorboards creak softly. As she passes, she can hear her father in his office. She hesitates. He does not come out to investigate, so on she goes to the kitchen. To find the paring knife. She holds the blade up. It would be good to let the pressure out. One cut would do it. Then there's a harsher thought: *Do it, you deserve to be punished.* She recognises a voice from her dream. She reveals her wrist. She can see thin blue lines and the humps of slender bones under the blanched flesh. *One cut. One cut and it would all be over; like lancing a boil, the pain would lessen. One cut. That's all.* Her thoughts are cajoling now.

Then she hears a scratchy shriek from the garden. She glances up. A gull hopping from webbed foot to webbed foot in some kind of rain dance. She looks back at the blade against her pallid skin and throws the knife away from her, into the cutlery tray. What is she thinking of? This is a sure sign of madness. She feels cold, suddenly aware of her bare feet and her thin nightdress. She quickly slams shut the drawer and hurries back to her bedroom. She wraps herself in her duvet. She will sleep now. She will tell no-one. It was an aberration brought on by bad dreams. She crashes into a slumber, a solid and airless vault from which she eventually returns unrested.

'Isn't it time you were going? I thought you were meeting what's-his-name.' What her mother means is, won't you please go out so I can entertain my bridge club without your dour face hanging around. Val Poole is looking immaculate if a little sweaty, overlaid as she is with make-up, gold jewellery and a tweedy twinset. Hannah sees her mother's disapproval of her patchwork cut-offs and baggy T-shirt. She agrees that she's on her way. Her disturbed night had made her think of Ben (a not infrequent thought) and this time she had given in and texted him to suggest meeting up. To her surprise he had replied promptly, suggesting coffee. She has somewhere to go. She'll be early. She'll saunter over.

The atmosphere in the house is oppressive, made worse by her mother's lingering Myrrh perfume. Outside the air is cooler than the scraped-clear skies and sparkling sun would have suggested. Hannah is glad she has bought a sweatshirt. As she makes her way down to the beach on the precipitous path, the summer day almost completely disappears. She can see it behind her, a glittering apparition; before her, white mists rolls in with the waves and curls its way across the sand, rubbing itself up the cliffs. The fret. Its dampness immediately insinuates itself down Hannah's spine, clings to her shins, so many ghostly arms of lost seafarers. The firm edge of the land is gone, she is balancing on a rim she cannot see. She walks more slowly, testing the ground with her feet before shifting her weight.

Dreams are nothing more than the sifting of the conscious through the sieve of the unconscious. They have meaning if she cares to give them meaning. She does not wish to. She wants to get through this year to accreditation with the minimum of fuss and back to London where she can disappear into the crowd. The fret coils around her, a cloak of ice. At least it hides her, hides what she fears to reveal. She knows she is a freak. She keeps it disguised, but, oh, what an effort it is, especially in the last few months. It was Dr Greene's fault, Dr Themis Greene: if she hadn't been there that day when she was, the rest would not have followed. Hannah would not have been so thrown off her centre as to have exposed her carefully concealed deviant behaviour. She stumbles on some loose gravel; it knocks against each other with the noise of billiard balls. The beach combed by the fret is deserted; she follows the concrete of the sea wall, which unravels itself each time she steps forward. A grey ribbon rolling out at the sand edge, leading her to where there will be people and bustle, to where she will have to don her disguise of normality so as to be acceptable.

She has to wait for Ben to turn up. The café is in town, so she had to leave the cloying fret and come into the broiling sun.

138

Eyes were upon her as she strode up the steps, through the steep gardens by the town hall, eyes that peeled back her skin to see the murk which lies beneath. Here, at least, seated in this cool room, her coffee successfully ordered and bought, she is unexceptional, another punter amongst the chattering pairs and groups around the other tables.

Ben arrives. He greets her warmly. They start by swapping news of what they have been doing. They have both been at a concert given by a local band and not seen each other. Hannah had been to a film with Agatha which Ben had wanted to see, though all she could tell him was that she had fallen asleep through most of it and Agatha had rated it. There's a pause and Hannah draws on the frothy dregs from her cup, looking away from his eyes, which are on her. He asks her how she is. She feels like crying. This impulse is coming upon her too often these days. She says something vague about the course and therapy being both intense and challenging. To which he nods; it had been that way for him too.

She is surprised. 'Then how did you manage to stick at it?'

'I bored people rigid telling them how awful it all was and got lots of support, well, therapy.'

'And you enjoy what you're doing? It was all worth it?'

Yes, definitely worth it. Yes, I enjoy my work. Sometimes it's hard when I'm with people who are particularly distressed and I have to question what use I can possibly be to them.'

Hannah nods, muttering her agreement.

'We never can know what we do, really; sometimes we get an inkling, but not always. It's hard when you're training cos you haven't been doing it enough to take the long view.'

'So it will get better?'

'Maybe. Or maybe you'll find it's not for you. I think only about four of us out of a training year of twelve are still doing it.'

'Thanks, that's encouraging,' she says dully, wondering how she ever thought talking to him might be helpful. Then he smiles and that does make a difference; he could even look faintly attractive if Hannah went for the hippy type. He apologises for being too sombre, one of his many faults. 'At least when you ask me how I am you, you listen to my response,' she replies, the impulse to weep returning.

He touches her very gently on the back of her hand resting on the table between them. 'Sounds like things are really tough for you. I'm all ears.'

'Oh, I don't know.' It feels too large to find something palatable enough to offer him. There's the dreams. There's her father's increasing reclusiveness, ill temper and frailty, which neither she nor Stephen seem able to tackle with either of their parents. There's the urge to ... she closes her eyes in an attempt to block out the image of what she nearly did this morning. Ben encloses her hand and this time does not move his away again. He repeats his reassurance that he's there to listen. And she finds herself talking about Aurora. A few times a week, Hannah has taken to going round in the mid-afternoon (when Max is often out) to ... what? Even she cannot define her motivation, except that it gets her out of her parents' house, and there's a desperation in Aurora which keeps calling her back. Sometimes they have quite ordinary conversations over a cup of tea Hannah now ensures she makes. Aurora offers a more tolerant view of her elderly neighbours, which helps Hannah see her parents with greater compassion than she generally manages. 'Wouldn't want to spend time alone with Stan, though,' Aurora had suddenly said once.

'What?'

'You know, bit creepy,' she continued, as if she wasn't talking about Hannah's father. Then, just as suddenly, she had jumped to another subject, as was her habit. But at other times, conversation was far from ordinary, and the house (though kept clean by more frequent visits from Rose) looked like it had been turned over by determined burglars. Then Hannah tries to put some order into the chaos as she listens to Aurora's wilder and wilder tales about Max. 'Her recent one is that he's had something to do with Dr Greene's murder. She says he's been violent in the past.'

140

'To her?' Ben asks worriedly.

'It's difficult to tell exactly what she means; to a previous girlfriend I think.'

Ben looks troubled.

'You've heard that too?'

'He can get a bit leary when he's had a few and I know he was in trouble when he was in his late teens, before he was with Aurora; got into a fight. I didn't know it was domestic violence.'

'It could have been that fight: women can get leary too when they get drunk.'

Ben shrugs. He doesn't look comfortable with this. He shakes his head when she asks if Max's been in trouble since he's known him. He asks if she's spoken to the police about it.

'It's a big leap from a lagered-up brawl to premeditated murder, don't you think? Anyway, Aurora also thinks Max and Oliver are both aliens.'

Ben half-smiles and then grimaces. 'Sounds like Aurora is struggling. Is she getting any help?'

'She's been to see Dr Courtney. When I suggested counselling to Max he was pretty displeased. Aurora says she's fine talking to me, and Rose.'

'A good team. Though I think you're right, she could benefit from some counselling too.' There's a pause. 'You know, I asked about you and you told me about Aurora. I'd still like to hear about you.'

A little thrill goes through her. He does have an appealing smile. And then she feels a clamp fix down on her jaw. *If I tell him anything, he'll leave too. I'll be too much for him and he'll make his excuses.* She gives one of her widest grins and says she's fine, she needs to get out more, that's all. Maybe they could have a meal together tonight, catch a film. He shakes his head: he has another commitment, in fact this week's rather busy. He begins to get out his diary; perhaps another time. *There, I knew it.* She pulls away her hand. 'Don't worry about it.' Checking the time on her phone, she says she has to go. As she gets up, he touches her sleeve and looks at her directly. 'I really

141

would like us to go out one evening, Hannah.' His voice sounds deceitfully genuine. She pauses for a heartbeat and then pulls away, saying, 'Text me,' as she leaves.

****

The heat has overreached itself. Last night it tipped into thunderstorms. Today the taupe clouds are spitting aimlessly. Theo is back to see Aurora. Having got to know Max, this time feels different. He is more reluctant to make the visit, initiated as it is by a call from Aurora, who told the desk sergeant taking her message that she is living with a murderer. DC Chesters, who is accompanying him, has already made it plain that he thinks they are walking into a 'domestic': Aurora is taking revenge, having lost an argument with her husband. Theo wishes for Harry's unobtrusive good sense. He wishes he didn't have to question a man he'd been to the pub with. He wishes he didn't know he's put this off for far too long; maybe with grim consequences, if Max's suspected violence has spread to hitting his wife. Most of all, he wishes he and Ben hadn't drowned their sorrows in quite so much red wine last night. He doesn't remember what Ben's sorrows were, but recalls talking too much about Lawrence.

He trudges up the front path, Chesters, like an overgrown whippet, at his shoulder. Theo's neck twinges painfully. It is Hannah who opens the door. She is wearing no make-up. Theo hasn't seen her face looking so bare, so vulnerable, before. There is a faint fan of acne over her cheekbones, her skin getting used to being exposed. Her hair has no highlights in it, undyed it is a rich brown; it is tousled instead of flattened. Her pale lips form an imploded line when she sees the two policemen. She hangs on to the door as if considering whether to keep them out. Chesters begins to say who they are and what they want. 'I know all that,' she interjects swiftly. She addresses Theo as 'Theo' (has she got that from hearing Lawrence talk about him?) then substitutes 'Sergeant Akande'. She says she doesn't think it's a good idea for them to come in: Aurora isn't herself. The reluctant

Chesters perks up. He demands her name, advises her she doesn't want to be risking a charge of perverting the course of justice. Theo silently curses the cramming Chesters has done for his sergeant exams and intervenes, promising Hannah he just wants to reassure himself that Aurora is OK. 'I hear she's not been well,' he adds. 'And you've been trying to support her; maybe we could be of assistance.' Though remaining wary of his Dixon-of-Dock-Green approach, Hannah is tempted by his offer of aid: Theo can see it in the tired droop around her tense eyes and mouth. She lets them in.

Aurora is in the sitting room. She is looking better than Theo expected and he sees Hannah's hand in this. Aurora is dressed in jeans and a pretty floral top, her hair neatly brushed back into a gold-coloured clasp, her face a deep bronze after the recent sun. Only the red lines clawed across the whites of her eyes speak of something different. Hannah offers coffee, which, as usual, Chesters accepts, and so Theo decides he can allow himself one: he could do with the caffeine. Aurora says she'll have a herbal tea and invites them to sit. She doesn't immediately speak. Theo reminds her she rang in and adds that they are here to help if they can.

'Are you wired?' she asks.

'I'm sorry?'

'Wired up. Have you got tape recorders?'

He shakes his head.

'Only they're listening, listening to every word I say, through your wires.'

'We don't have any wires.'

Chesters asks the obvious question Theo is avoiding. 'Who are "they"?'

'Them.' Aurora glances ceilingward. 'The ones who have taken my Max and baby and brought those imposters here instead. It's the imposter Max who did it, he killed Dr Greene.' Aurora is gabbling quietly. 'I can't say more, they'll hear me.'

'Right.' Chesters' body is on the point of rising from the chair. Perhaps it is the smell of real coffee brewing that keeps him rooted where he is. He rolls his eyes at Theo.

Theo ignores him. He says, 'We're not wired and we've swept the premises for devices. Those that were here aren't working right now; we've got maybe an hour before they start listening again. Why don't you tell me what you know about the imposter Max?' Chesters gives a stagey cough. Theo continues to keep his focus on Aurora.

'Are you certain?' she says.

'Absolutely.'

She talks then and some of what she says fits in with what he already knows. Her Max had a loan from Dr Greene. It had slipped her mind when they spoke before because as far as she knew it had been paid back or written off. It hadn't been, but she only found this out recently, from the Imposter Max. She'd also only discovered in the last week that her Max had a meeting with Dr Greene on the day she died. Aurora'd been trying to remember what had happened. He'd gone out in the afternoon and hadn't come back until the evening. She'd been asleep; when she'd woken up he'd already returned, out of sorts. They'd argued, he'd put the washing machine on for the clothes he'd been wearing and hadn't bothered with any in the basket which needed doing. He'd been overly angry when she'd pointed this out to him. She now thinks maybe that was when the switch was made, to the imposter.   'Now, Aurora.' Hannah had entered with a tray and at this moment puts it down, serving out the drinks. 'I thought we weren't going to talk about that to the police.'

'But you know it's true, Hannah, he's so different these days.' Aurora's voice whines a little.

'I didn't know him before,' Hannah replies tightly. 'And having a baby is a big change for anyone. Tell them about the diary entry, about the hammer.'

The other woman takes a sip of tea and then does as she is bid. Max hadn't said where he was going that Sunday and she had assumed it was to work. She'd only found out about the meeting with Dr Greene from the diary.

'He's not mentioned it in all these months?' Theo asks.

She shakes her head and continues to drink her tea.

He takes a mouthful of his coffee, enjoying the warm, milky flavour, then he prompts her about the hammer.

'Hammer?' She appears confused. She gazes pleadingly over to Hannah. She responds that Aurora had told her yesterday the hammer was missing from the toolbox in the garage. She had looked and also could not find it.

'And there used to be a hammer?' Theo questions.

Aurora nods, calling on Hannah to back her up. 'I don't know,' says Hannah. 'How would I know? I've never looked in their toolbox before. All I can say is it's not there currently.'

'It was done with a hammer, wasn't it?' Aurora asks. 'Hannah said it was.'

Theo says nothing. *How does she know? It wasn't in the papers.* He doesn't get a chance to ask.   There's a hint of a whimper from upstairs. Aurora is on her feet, saying she has to go. Chesters tells her to stop, far too harshly for Theo's liking, and she freezes. Hannah more gently suggests Oliver will be alright for a moment. She strokes the other woman's arm. Making a mental note for Chesters' next appraisal, Theo explains they will have to search the house and they will be speaking to Max. Both of these appear to shock Aurora further and she pleads with them not to. 'If they find out what I've been saying, they'll … they'll take me apart.'

Theo cuts off Chesters' enquiry about who they are with a withering stare. He says, 'We'll protect you.'

'You will?' Aurora had slumped down onto the couch and then jumped up at the baby's more audible cry. At this moment she is stretched out between two imperatives. Theo repeats his guarantee of protection and she is released to rush out of the room. He expresses concern over how Aurora will cope when he sends his officers over to help Chesters with the search and while he is questioning Max. Hannah says she'll sort it out with Rose and maybe get Aurora's parents up.

'You don't think he did it, do you? Max?' she asks sadly. 'I mean, Lawrence had a drink with him.'

Theo gulps down the last of his coffee. He can feel the heat of his cheeks rouging, at the casual utterance of Lawrence's name. And there's something else: he recognises (not for the first time) the intertwining of Hannah's and Lawrence's lives, and he's none too comfortable with it. 'I cannot be certain either way,' he says briskly.

And he's no nearer being certain three hours and twenty-three minutes later. He has been questioning Max Harris for one hour and twenty-three minutes and he's no closer to finding answers. A note has just been sent in: no hammer has been found at the house and Aurora is claiming the clothes she saw Max go out in on that Sunday are no longer in the wardrobe. Reggie Harvey is once again in attendance and he and his client are competing for the 'Most outrageous tie' award. Max's, with its splashes of lime, lemon and strawberry, hangs down to the second button of his lavender shirt now open at the neck. He is more florid than ever, his face solid as steel, his eyes narrowed and his mouth set. He is saying very little. He won't say where he was for those hours he was out on the 22nd of February; it's a private matter, but he was not with Dr Greene. Yes, he'd had an appointment with her, only he'd cancelled it, they'd spoken on the phone, everything was worked out between them. If Theo thinks he is better off with Dr Greene dead then he can think again: Max had nothing on paper about their new agreement, so he is having to deal with Penny Greene, which is proving more tricky. Dr Greene had appeared pretty desperate for the money. They could try looking into her financial affairs for a murderer. Yes, there was a hammer in the toolbox. He has no idea why it's not there at this point in time. Folding up the note, Theo asks him about the clothes. Max replies they were thrown because they'd got irreparably spoilt.

'During your jaunt out on the 22nd?'

Reggie lifts a finger, suggesting caution. Max shrugs and says nothing, hunkering further down into the bulk of his shoulders.

Theo lets his breath whistle out between his teeth. 'You know, Max, it would make things an awful lot easier if you would say where you went.'

'It's none of your business.'

'It is when there's been a murder.'

'I didn't murder her,' Max replies forcefully, clenching his fists as if he could cheerfully murder the man across the table from him, or, at least, give him a good thumping. Reggie lifts his cautioning finger again. Max grumphs.

'I think, Sergeant,' Reggie says in his cultured, conciliatory tones, 'we've been round this particular field of enquiry a number of times. My client has given his answers. Perhaps it might be time to take a break?'

Theo wonders if Reggie has some kind of engagement to get to, a charity dinner perhaps, one which entailed him bringing out his crimson cummerbund and spotted bow tie. Maybe he's right, though, they do seem to be going round in circles. He doesn't have enough to charge Max, even if he felt inclined to do so.

'Who set you up to this?' Max asks, his voice thick, menacing.

'I can't divulge sources, you know I can't,' Theo replies peaceably.

'It was her, wasn't it?' Max can barely contain his shouting despite Reggie's warning hand clamped briefly on his wrist. 'I don't know what's come over her, she's … she's not making any sense any more. I don't care what Dr Courtney says, Aurora, my wife, she's going off her rocker.' In contrast to his blustering, Max's face is crumpling. 'You can't believe what she's saying, Theo, Detective Sergeant, you can't. She's … she's not well.' Theo is considering some calming phrases and then cutting his suspect loose on caution when Max finishes with force: 'Wait 'til I fucking get home, I'll have a word with her, get this straightened out.'

Reggie closes his eyes momentarily and shakes his head. He's probably calculating he's now on target to miss the hors d'oeuvres.

Theo sits back. He can feel the tension from the woman officer next to him. He wants to yell at Max, tell him what an idiot he's been. Instead he flexes his hands and then clasps them in front of him. 'I'm afraid I can't let you go home, Max. If I let you go, you'll be under caution and I'll have to insist you go elsewhere to stay for a while.'

'Not go home? Not see Oliver? You're insane. You can't stop me.' Those fists hit the table with a resounding thump.

'I can.' Theo keeps his voice level. 'And you can either reside in the cells until I get the necessary orders, or we can come to an amicable agreement.' Those fists were about to take flight in Theo's direction and Reggie is having to put some effort into his restraining hand. Theo suggests they take a short break, ends the interview, shuts off the taping equipment and tells his assistant to follow him out of the room. In the corridor, drinking insipid machine-egested coffee, he notices a slight tremor in his fingers. Those fists could do real damage. *With a hammer to Dr Greene? To Aurora?* If he does let Max go, he would have to find a way of backing up Hannah and get some patrols to keep an eye on Aurora, perhaps even on Max's parents and sister. *Maybe I should hold on to him. Could I really trust him not to attack his wife, or run, his baby with him?* Reggie (obviously determined not to miss his main course) helps him with his indecision. Max has agreed to go quietly to a B&B. Reggie will take him there and the owner is an ex-policeman who isn't averse to acting as an informal holding pen. They can organise injunctions as necessary in the morning. Theo consents with some relief. Max looks downcast as he leaves. He becomes distraught when he is told, no he cannot send a text for Oli. Reggie leads him away to a taxi.

Theo still has some work to do. He talks to Hannah who reluctantly consents to stay in the house with Aurora until she's agreed to her parents coming. Hannah also (even more reluctantly) says he can contact Ben for further backup. 'If you insist, only I'm sure Rose and I will do fine,' she says stiffly. He makes the call to Ben anyway, asking him to pop by, explaining Max is having to stay away from the house for a while. Used to asking the minimum of questions when circumstances demand it, Ben says he will. Theo then organises for hourly patrols to pass by the requisite streets. To finish, he makes sure all the fingerprints from the room where Dr Greene was murdered are finally sent off for processing.

Chapter 23

The grey rag of cloud is torn away and there's an aluminium hole in the black sky. It would be possible to tumble right through. Hannah tenses her torso to prevent herself from doing so. Ben must have discerned her slight movement. He takes his arm from her waist and asks her if she's OK. She says of course she is. She doesn't want anything — least of all her errant notions — to spoil it all. She thinks she's done a good job of projecting her acceptable side; she won't allow herself to upset things now.

She had been put out, the evening Max was taken into custody, when Ben had arrived, like some kind of knight in shining armour, like the little women couldn't cope without his intervention. He did prove adept at talking to Aurora, however, putting alternatives to her alien-abduction theories without annihilating her, and even getting her to accept other realities might be possible. Hannah was further mollified when he took her part in urging Aurora to take some sleeping pills and then go back to Dr Courtney's the following week, a move Rose and Aurora were less than keen on. Though it was seeing the relationship he had with Rose which softened her the most. She found the tight coil inside her easing a little in the glow of the warmth with which they treated each other. It occurred to her that this was how it should be between mother and child, not the frosty disinterest which abounded in her parents' home. And she giggled at Rose's capacity to tease Ben away from his tendency to pomposity with a gently delivered, 'I wasn't aware we'd had need of the cavalry, until you turned up to inform us.'

Aurora had taken her prescribed medication and she had slept, for a fourteen-hour stretch, awaking less agitated. They had managed to agree that her parents would come tomorrow and her mother would go to the GP with her. They had also found a way, with the intervention of Max's mother and sister, for father and son to spend a short time together. When Ben had suggested dinner, Hannah had been comfortable with leaving Aurora on her own. Hannah had felt excitement at getting ready; she hadn't expected to. She had trained her curls into an iron-rich waterfall cascading down her neck, held in place by a black, large-toothed grip. She chose to wear her black dress, tight-fitting until it flares out across her hips into a skirt which stops minutely above the knee. She matched it with opal earrings and pendant and an umber linen jacket (praying the rain would not return). She applied the minimum of make-up, concentrating on glossing up her lips, and forsook her three-inch black patent stilettos, putting on instead some flat strappy sandals in dull bronze. Their outing (she dared not call it a date) had lived up to all this attention. The conversation had flowed. About work, how tough it is to retain confidence when working as a therapist. About Labour's routing in the recent local elections, Hannah's boredom with the whole thing causing a flicker of tension between them. He sounded a might too like her father barking on about democracy and what large swathes of the world wouldn't give to have the opportunity she has to vote. 'But it makes no difference whatever I vote, the politicians still mess up,' she snapped. 'You'd know the difference if you were in a country where you couldn't vote,' he retorted. They found more even ground with books, music, film; and the red wine she was drinking gave him an ever more attractive demeanour. She invited him back (her parents having decamped to Stephen's for their twice yearly 'fortnight in purgatory' as her father put it). They wandered up the Esplanade, the dark sea shushing the night, the moon sheening the silhouetted leaves and tree trunks. They shared comic snippets from Douglas Adams and Monty Python. Their shoulders and hands touched. He weighted the centre of her back with his hand, anchoring her from floating away — until he removed it on her almost imperceptible inflection. Now she reaches up and touches his face, he turns and her lips follow her fingers to his mouth. He responds with a long-drawn-out kiss, pulling her closer. She can smell him, his warming skin, his pulsing blood, beneath the laundered cotton and the scentless soap. The connection through her lips slips down her body with a tender hum. They move apart. She feels

151

the possibility of something more; it crackles around them in the plush night.

The house is in darkness and she doesn't bother with turning on the lights. The moon, in any case, is paling the shadows. They kiss again in the hallway. She pulls him towards the stairs. He kisses her neck from behind and then down her arm, drawing back her jacket sleeve, lips on flesh. He stops at her wrist, straightens, her hand in his. She tries to move them onto the steps, only he is holding back. She pauses, scanning his face. 'What?'

'Wait.'

What for? Why? She tries again to draw him after her. He shakes his head, smiling. Laughing? Laughing at her? She feels whatever has been keeping her together during the evening quiver and begin to collapse. *He doesn't, after all, want me.* She loses all her energy and sits heavily on the stairs, chin cupped in her hands.

He leans forward and strokes her hair down to her shoulders. 'This is a bit fast. For me.'

She jerks his hand away, though it was soothing. 'You don't like me. You don't find me attractive.' She tells herself sternly, *You idiot.*

He sits down beside her. 'Of course I do.'

'Then what's stopping you?' She looks round at his face.

'Hannah, I like you. Only, you're … you're … I think you're a bit fragile right now. I don't want to take advantage of you.'

She moves closer and offers her lips, 'Please, take advantage.'

He chuckles. 'No.' He kisses her to the side of her mouth.

She feels little, remembers sitting on stairs as a child. *What was I doing there? Sent there as a punishment?* She can't be sure. Her words come tumbling out as a wail. 'Why don't you want me?' The gloom is creeping across the floor, ready to engulf her. She wails again, a tearless cry emanating from her plexus, which is being ripped open to let the noise out. 'Hannah, Hannah, come on.' It's Ben's soothing voice at first, then there

152

are others, harsher, cackling. The witches, they'd been executed on this spot, their ghosts are forming themselves out of the coats hanging by the front door. Her name repeated again, whispered through time, pulling her up and into the well formed by the moon in the sky. 'Here, drink this.' She's being offered poison, she tries to push it away, but the witch won't have it. 'You'll feel better.'

She shoves it away and shouts to be heard.

'Hannah, focus on my voice, it's Ben, I'm not going to hurt you.'

An orangey glow begins to shoo back the night and its beasts, her hiccupping for oxygen is easing, in the lamplight she can see the room around her. The living room with its cabbage greens against the yellow walls, the bookshelves, horrid dark-wood rococo-style coffee table, they all begin to take shape. She is perched on the edge of the sofa with Ben beside her holding a half-empty glass of water, a dark patch on the front of his oatmeal-coloured shirt. 'You're wet,' she says, reaching out and checking.

He says the glass had got knocked and gives it to her. The water douses the fever in her mouth and throat. He begins to say they have to talk, about what's just happened; and as she remembers some of their recent exchange, the fire transfers to her cheeks. She starts to apologise, saying she quite understands, she's not his type. She has to make him understand, *I'm normal*. He puts his finger to her mouth, silencing her, telling her that's not what he meant. 'I think you're having a hard time, right now I think it would help you if you talked some, about how you're feeling.'

She laughs, surprised when it comes out as more of a croak, says she's fine and she doesn't know what he's on about. She wants him to get out of the way, leave her be. Anxiety catches at the back of her gullet. She's tired, she tells him, needs to go to bed. Is he staying or leaving?

He catches hold of her left arm, his thumb and middle finger braceleting her wrist, says something about self-harming,

153

it's serious, repeats that they need to talk, more forcefully this time.

'What are you wittering about? I don't self-harm.'

He's peeling back her sleeve, urging her to look, asking her how often she cuts herself.

'Get off me, get the fuck off me!' she yells, pulling away from him.

He lets go. 'Hannah, listen.'

'No,' she says loudly. 'You listen, I'm fucking tired and I'm going to bed. You do what you want. See if I care.' She gets up and walks determinedly out of the room, only by the time she starts to climb the stairs she's found her legs are numb and shaky. She doesn't want to be on her own: she's scared of what might be waiting for her upstairs, what might be coiled on the landing ready to strike. 'Ben.'

'I'm here.'

'I don't want to be alone.' He promises to stay, he says the sofa, she says in the guest room below hers, it's closer.

'I'm frightened.'

'I know.' He puts his arm around her waist and supports her as she begins to slowly ascend.

Chapter 24

Aurora sees the moon — an ivory button in the corseted sky — from Oliver's bedroom window. He's fed and bathed and in his cot. Normally she would leave him now, with only the dim night light on, saying curtly, 'Goodnight, Oliver, time to sleep.' Only she doesn't want to. Hannah is out with Ben. Hadn't she seen the spark between them when they met here? In that other life she used to have? She stares out at the dark navy which is resting heavily on the treetops and roofs. An aeroplane had fallen off that wadded cloth, its thread snipped, inexplicably, on the far side of the earth. Hundreds dead, unknown to her; still she wants to weep for them. Or perhaps for herself, and maybe Max, chess pieces on the opposite corners of the board. She hears a snicker from behind her. She turns. Oliver is awake and languidly playing footy with his blanket. Max would love that. The baby holds out his open palm to her and then scrunches up his fingers. He repeats this a few times: come, come, come. She pulls a chair over and sits by him. 'Aren't you tired, little man?' She lets her thumb be taken in his fist. She asks him what he wants. He smiles, or maybe it's merely wind. His gaze is on her. She cannot go now. She is leaning forward, tense. What should she do? 'When I was young I would always tell myself stories to get myself off to sleep.' Hannah Leigh's words come back to her.

'Once upon a time,' she begins slowly, not sure where this will lead her. She pauses. The child's breathing is heavy produced by the contraction and relaxation of all the muscles in his small body. He cannot understand what she is saying, only absorb her meaning, as clay takes in paint or glaze. She pictures herself as a baby: she was a doughy little one too, she has seen the many photos. She was the much longed-for baby, the much-prized child. Her parents haven't said much about it; she has had to piece together their tale. She restarts quietly. 'Once upon a time, in a far-off country, there was a king and queen. The king and queen were as handsome and as beautiful as anyone could have wished. He came from a kingdom across the sea and had skin the colour of tea. His eyes were as coal and his hair was black and wiry, encircling his head with the cut of a monk's. She was taller than him, bigger-boned, a native of the northern regions where they had come to live, with her paler features and hair down to her waist the shade of the fur of a field mouse.'

Aurora hesitates. *What next?* Slowly she continues. 'The king and queen loved each other, had overcome opposition to their love and marriage in order to be together. Neither of their families was happy with their offspring's choice, preferring the match should come from within their own peoples. As the years passed, however, and they saw the love the king and queen held for each other, the families became more reconciled to what had happened. Love, so it seemed, knew not the bounds of nationhood and race. Others in the kingdom were less forgiving and expressed their distaste with harsh whispers and glances, the occasional letter written with poisoned ink or tipped rubbish on the front doorstep. In general, though, when the subjects came to know the king and queen, they could not but come to admire, respect and even like them.

'The seasons turned. Not always as expected; sometimes there were hot dry days in winter and cold wet ones in summer, or leaves were yellow in spring while boughs budded in autumn. Even so, these were mere blips in the usual rotation of the world, nothing to cause too great consternation. The king and queen worked hard in their GP surgery, spent long hours in their separate consulting rooms listening to the woes of humankind, feeling the brittleness of human life. Some said it was better to be seen by the king: his hands retained the warmth of his home country and when he looked closely at you healing came directly from those dark eyes. Others preferred the queen's ability to get things done, an X-ray brought forward, a consultant found and briefed quickly, test results in days rather than weeks. Either way, the king and queen's surgery was always full. There was one sorrow, however, one rent in the tapestry: the queen could not carry a baby to term.'

Oliver gives out a quiet snort. Aurora sees that his eyes are closed and his neck and limbs are relaxed. She doesn't know when he nodded off. She tucks the blanket over his feet. One of them twitches: he is already running in his dreams.

Chapter 25

Surprisingly it is Clarke who notices and kindly enquires after her, cutting short James's rather too graphic description of his antics with his new 'lady', since he walked out on his wife of twenty-five years a mere three weeks previously. And Clarke doesn't take 'fine' as an answer. Everyone is quiet, the room is stuffy, the clouds Hannah can see through the window are charged with rain and yet do not let loose their load. Clarke smiles encouragingly. She had apologised to him some time back and he had waved it away, saying sorry is an overused word; in his opinion there are no such things as mistakes, only learning opportunities. And she has learnt something: she has only text Ben twice a day, making an effort to keep her panic and recriminations out of her missives. His responses have been minimal. Breaking the rules agreed at the beginning of the course, she has her phone on 'vibrate' in her pocket in case he replies to her latest suggestion for meeting up — it feels leaden against her thigh. 'You have seemed down recently,' Agatha says. 'What is it?' Hannah is a lobster thrown live into a broiling pan. Sweat pricks at her underarms. She begins to roll up her sleeves, then remembers why she cannot. 'I've put myself out there,' Agatha continues. 'We all have, it's not fair that you should be purely a voyeur.' She is red-eyed from crying about not being allowed to grieve her husband's passing enough because everyone had expected her to get on with it, to cope, because she's a coper. She's looking vaguely dishevelled, breaking her 'be prefect' script, as she explained earlier. Clarke defends Hannah's right to say as little as she wants and he and Agatha squabble around the point of group process if some people choose not to participate or even lie.

'I've never lied,' says Hannah, piqued.

'There's lying by omission,' says Agatha, and both Clarke and Tina chime in with that not being fair.

'So what's stopping you being here, Hannah?' asks Fred in his languid way.

'I am here,' Hannah says, irritated.

'Physically, maybe. You've never properly landed emotionally. What's so scary about doing that?'

She looks around at the faces turned towards her, she's stuck in a magician's spider's web, she has to answer the riddles to gain her release. She comes back to focusing on the second button down on Fred's flowered silk shirt. 'I guess ... I guess I'm just not really sure this is for me.'

Tina and Agatha protest in unison, she's doing so well in her written work (true) and on her placement (less true than it was, though she hasn't admitted this to anyone apart from herself yet; she's losing her capacity to stay with her clients for the hour).

Fred's voice cuts through the chorus. 'You're not going to ever be sure unless you give yourself permission to commit once and for all. Tell us about your nightmares.'

'Pardon?'

'You've been having nightmares, tell us about them.'

How does he know? His blue eyes turn to lumps of basalt. Answer the riddle, Hannah, and you'll get to escape. 'I've a rag stuffed in my mouth, covering my nose, I can't breathe properly, something is constricting my chest.' Her fear rises up her throat, mercury up the neck of a thermometer. She sees herself battering Dr Greene. She has to delete that out of her mind. 'I can't talk,' she says, squeezing the words out. 'I can't.'

'Who's stopping you?'

Faceless, nameless people. She drops her head.

'What would happen if you did talk?' asks Clarke gently.

'Everyone would blow up,' she replies quietly. 'Everybody would be destroyed.'

'Wow, that's big.'

'Maybe you'd find,' Agatha says reasonably, 'it doesn't destroy everyone if you do talk. You don't have any evidence it will.'

Hannah gazes up at the other woman. Agatha's face is looking decidedly haggard today, her hair is dull. Hannah thinks she would have done better not to fight her script with quite so much vehemence. 'I know,' Hannah says flatly. 'I know what will happen.'

'You may like to think about how that belief serves you.' Fred's tone is sharp as he continues, 'And what you gain from wasting my time and yours.'

'Ouch,' says Clarke. But before he can go on, all their attentions are caught by Tina's sniffing gaining in volume. When prompted she wails that if Hannah isn't going to make it to being a counsellor then she certainly won't because she's such a klutz at it all. What finally transpires through much sobbing and hiccuping and with much encouragement is that she's going to have to give up the course anyway because her fiancé has just told her he has got a new job in Chesterfield and is insisting she move with him. Enquiries follow from everyone in the room. Couldn't she stay behind until she finishes? (This from Clarke.) Couldn't she find another course to go to? (This from Hannah.) Didn't her fiancé think to ask her before applying for the job? (This from Agatha.) 'You follow your heart,' says James. 'Love is more important than any training.'

'I do love him.' Tina's garnet eyes glitter wetly in her round, swollen face. 'I do want to be married.'

'Which is it?' Agatha mutters tersely.

'If he loves you,' Hannah says, glad to have the spotlight off her, 'he'll help you finish your course, if that's what you want.'

'Of course it is,' Tina replies swiftly. 'Only he's been against me going into this type of work since that thing with Dr Greene. He thinks it's dangerous, working with clients.'

'I've survived twenty-seven years in the business,' Fred says mildly.

'I know.' Tina smiles secretively. 'Only he wants children. We both do.'

'Tina, you're twenty-four,' Agatha bursts out.

James says he had his first when he was eighteen. 'It's good to have 'em when you're young yourself.' And there's a brief interlude of no it isn't/yes it is between Agatha and James, until Fred calls time. Clearly peevish, he suggests that both Tina and Hannah consider their priorities, then he stomps out of the room. A waft of less-stale air steals in through the open door. Hannah closes her eyes, supping it up.

Chapter 26

Alone in the house except for the cub, Aurora has slept fitfully. Now she is awake again, restless; the wind has snapped off a piece of the tree in the street below the window. It is midnight, the hour tired princesses return to their rooms with holes in their shoes, excited to tell of their adventures. She cannot stay in bed. The door to the child's room is ajar; she can see the shape of his stern jaw by the glow of the night light. She sits by his bed, listening to the tuneless yawning of the gale outside. She is thinking about her parents' story. They had each other, clung to each other through all that time, holding out against disapproval, loyal when faced by troubles. She and Max had held each other together like that once. How did they — she — come to let go? Her fingers stroke the child's forehead. It is warm, warmer than it should be. She realises that he is uneasy in his slumber, she remembers how her voice had quietened him the previous night. She speaks softly. 'Once upon a time in a country not so far away from ours, a princess was born to a king and queen. She was named Aurora, the goddess of new dawns. Owing to a spell cast too long ago to be remembered, her days were not hung with gold, diamonds and crystal glittering in the candlelight, their reflections reflected by silvered glass, on and on, until it seemed like they might reach the moon. The princess would never find a door to the attic in which were stored spinning wheels by the hundred on which to prick her finger. She would never enter an enchanted wood nor lose herself in a maze. Instead her domain was a three-bedroom semi-detached, with a through lounge downstairs and a neat garden out the back.

'The day the princess was born was mild and sunny, which would not be surprising if it had not been in December and for weeks before and after storms raged. It was as if a calm, honeyed eye had watched over her coming. She was long awaited; her parents' desire for a child had been accompanied by much suffering. Small wonder, then, that she was held close by both of them.

'To receive all the nurturing and attention she needed, there was only one thing that the princess had to ensure: she had to stay well. As doctors, the king and queen dealt with every kind of disease and wound in a sympathetic, matter-of-fact manner. When it came to the princess, however, they could not bear the thought of damage coming to her. The first time she caught a childish tummy bug, the king and queen's world was turned upside down, the sky and stars crashed to earth, while trees became uprooted and insects crept under rocks for safety. The king and queen cried, holding each other, distraught, as their daughter puked, believing, truly, that she was about to be taken away from them. Their hands shook as they cleaned her up with cloths soaked by their own tears. The princess's first knee scrape was treated as if it were a compound fracture and balancing on walls was banned for the foreseeable future.

'The princess was not dull-witted, so she quickly learnt that illness and injury was a calamity which knew no bounds. The air became thick with guilt and blame like it was a smog. Though it was unclear to the princess from where it emanated, it was obvious where it came to settle: on her shoulders.' Oliver curls over and whimpers in his sleep. Aurora touches his cheek. 'My poor baby.' *The other thing the princess had to do to ensure love was graft — graft hard.*

****

Hannah had gazed at the horizon, which was cut across and across by a dozen dark daggers, then she saw it bleed white electric discharge. She heard its agony roll across the aluminium sea, then felt its corpulent tears on her own cheeks. The bellows grew louder, the clouds spewed lightning, she was soaked through by the time she went back into the house. Telling herself what a fool she was, she changed into some trackie bottoms and a sweatshirt and towelled her hair. A yellow glow outside the windows and thunder stamping across the roof tiles announced the arrival of the woman more than the front doorbell.

She is in white, what could be a bridal dress, torn and muddied at the hem. Her blonde tresses fan out over her shoulders; the tips are dipped in blood. Her face is elfin, painted over with make-up that sparkles. She is shorter than Hannah, slighter, yet there's something in her demeanour that rebukes denial. Anyway, she says the enchanted word 'Ben'. She has a message from Ben, or, at least, that's what Hannah thinks she says. Once inside she demands wine as a ransom and plies too much of the damson liquid to Hannah. It infuriates the bees fidgeting in her head. One or two of them slip into her throat and down into her stomach, all the while getting angrier. She tries to insist the younger woman tell her what Ben has said. She only smiles in return. Her finger collects a drop of red wine from the bottle's lip as she finishes pouring once more. She slips her pinkie's pointed tip into her mouth, regarding Hannah from under long, curved, dark eyelashes. Then, draining her glass and taking it with a full bottle of wine, she goes towards the stairs, asking if this is where the bedroom is.

'Who are you?' asks Hannah.

'Maya,' comes the answer, moving towards the heavens.

Theirs is no prim first kiss. Lips meet with bruising intimacy and tongues force teeth apart, hands clasp roughly at shoulders and breasts. And metres away at the bottom of the cliffs, the sea throws itself onto broken shells. Hannah tries to draw back, to let go, suddenly aware of a piece of metal's capacity to burn. Yet she is held in a vice. Their subsequent embraces, the smouldering embers licking up through her body, scramble what is left of her senses.

****

'Once upon a time.' The storm has passed and the sky is becoming paler from the east. The baby sleeps, air whining through constricted airways. The house creaks, but she knows it is not something malevolent approaching. She settles the blanket around the infant again and strokes the soft skin of his wrist. She continues: 'In a place and age not so different from our own, there lived a princess named Aurora, the princess of new dawns. She may have been a princess but she was expected to work, at school, doing chores at home and, once she was in her teens, in her parents' GP surgery.

'She looked on her parents' patients with pity and fear, which mixed together added up to a fair amount of loathing. They were, after all, sick, which was, she knew as surely as she understood that red blood cells carry oxygen, a failing, proof that you had somehow lost control. There was nothing to be more abhorred than a body which had become so devious. One evening half a year after her fourteenth birthday, she told her parents at dinner that she had changed her mind about helping out in the surgery. Both her parents laid down their cutlery and looked at her. The queen took a long drink of water before asking the simple question, "Why?" Perhaps if she had explained it all to them properly, they would have accepted her decision. But under their twinned gaze, she felt a new emotion stirring, which made her want to shout, to kick at the table legs; she did not know it was called obstinacy. So she gave a reply which even she could see was wholly inadequate: "Because I don't want to." Her mother said that there were times when everyone had to do things they did not want to do and, indeed, the majority of the population did jobs they hated for the majority of their lives. She went back to eating. Her father was more conciliatory, said they could really do with her help. He continued to hold her with the warmth from his coal eyes. So the princess quelled her impulse to set her mouth and cross her arms and she acquiesced to her parents. All along that little core of obstinacy grew a thicker and thicker shell.'

****

Morning only slowly filters through into Hannah's consciousness. Her head aches, she feels sick, her mouth is dry, her eyes are pasted together. It is when she finally prises them open and sees the white dress and blonde wig abandoned on the floor that something of the previous night oozes into her mind. She can smell Maya's musk of wild wormwood and gardenia hanging heavily around her. She wants to crawl under the duvet and never come out. *How could I have done any of that?* She berates herself, a fist to her temple, hard enough to mark. The covers are dragged back and an imp stands there with a chipped mug of steaming liquid. Her short-cropped hair is dyed maroon, she is wearing something that looks like one of Stan Poole's dress shirts. *Has she been in my parents' bedroom?* Her bare feet are tiny, the glittery black polish is chipped. *Was it like that last night?* Her large eyes are bruised with badly removed heavy make-up. 'Have a brew,' she says brightly, clambering back onto the bed and spilling most of the milky drink in the process. Hannah takes it from her and sips it; it is cold and too sweet, it almost makes her gag.

'What have you been doing to yourself, honey?' For a moment Maya sounds like Rose. She gently smoothes the tender flesh on the side of Hannah's head. Then she asks for the tools for a manicure and pedicure and goes to help herself to them before she is given permission to do so. As she removes polish, buffs the skin on her feet, rubs in cream, files her nails and begins to apply some of Hannah's pearly-pink varnish, she reminisces about her and Ben. Friends since childhood, he was her protector. She even has an old photo she keeps in her purse. There's the two of them as kids, Ben looking scrawny in oversized jacket and wellies, wearing a black, pointed hat, his long, narrow hands too big for his childish arms. A diminutive Maya posing in flowing bluey-green robes. 'Fancy dress?' Hannah suggests.

'It was Sawhain,' Maya replies, absorbed by the picture.

'Sow-in?'

'Never mind,' the younger woman snaps, repossessing the images for herself, putting them back in her bag. Then she laughs. Her rowanberry lips curve, revealing her sharp white teeth. 'Ben and Maya, Maya and Ben,' she sing-songs. 'It's always been that way.' She puts her hand to the deep V of maple-syrup skin caught in the starched, virginal cloth of the shirt. Then she turns her dark eyes on Hannah. 'And it always will be.'

Hannah struggles not to drown herself in the bedcovers again. 'You said you had a message from him for me.'

'No, I don't think so. I don't think he's got anything to say to you.' Maya goes back to her beauty treatments.

'He said he would get in touch.' Hannah's voice is a piteous mew.

Maya shrugs. 'Aren't you getting up? You look like shit.'

Hannah does as she is bid. She is desperate for the toilet and for a shower. These completed she returns to the bedroom to find Maya has purloined some leggings and is gathering up her own clothes into one of Hannah's bags: her Fiorelli. 'You're going?' she says, anxiety scrabbling at the sandpaper in her throat.

'Maybe.' She sits at the desk, admiring the work she has done on her hands and feet. 'They don't think much of you, do they?'

'Who?' Hannah is sorting out what she is going to wear and only half listening.

'Your mum and dad. I went through every room—.'

'Every?' Hannah jerks upright.

Maya continues: 'I counted twenty-three photos of your brother; Stephen, isn't it? And there were two of you. One of those was with' (she emphasises the 'with') 'Stephen. Must piss you off.'

'Mind your own fucking business.' Hannah goes back to her dressing, having to move slowly. She can hear the other woman fiddling with things, opening drawers, moving books about. Hannah tenses.

'What's this?'

Hannah looks up. Maya is holding the journal she started at Izzie's instigation. Hannah lifts her shoulders and pushes them down again, an effort at nonchalance. Maybe if she pretends not to care Maya will relinquish it. She does not. She adopts a deep, overdramatic voice, and reads, 'I am feeling on edge, edgy, all my edges fraying, falling apart. Tatty, unsightly, my self unravels. Now I am a pile of undone thread, kinked, twisted, unsorted.' In her ordinary tone, Maya says, 'Aw, Hannah, how sweet. And what's this? You've filled a page with "I want" here, Hannah. What are you going on about? No, wait a moment.'

'Nooooo!' Hannah is suddenly springing at the younger woman, tearing at her, prising the notebook out of her hands, taking her so much by surprise that she manages to do it. Then she stands hugging it to her chest, panting.

Maya raises a tweezered eyebrow; her mouth is stilled in a pert O. Then she grins. 'I want Benedick Cartwright. I don't think so, Hannah.' She cackles.

'Shut up, just shut up.'

'You listen to me, Hannah, Ben belongs to Maya, you remember that. And he doesn't want you anyway. I saw those scars last night all up your arm. You're a fucking nutter.'

Hannah is shaking, tremors belting her spine. 'Stop, stop, stop it! Get out!'

Maya lets out a long sigh and then in one languid movement stands. 'If that's what you want.'

No reply: Hannah can't get words past her teeth.

Maya saunters towards the door. 'I'll be off, then.' She pauses.

Hannah is a ladybird trapped in a black widow spider's web.

'OK, if I'm leaving, it's for ever.' Still she doesn't move.

And something in that last word brings Hannah round, she grabs at Maya's wrist, only the fragile joint slips from her fingers, the flitting of a bat's wing. So she has to follow, gasping at air and stumbling down the stairs. 'Maya, wait.' She finds herself looking into eyes the colour of cats' fur. She remembers the kisses — not light summer kisses these — they tasted of the smoke from winter firewood, of salt, burned from the sea, of molten lava pouring from the centre of the earth. She feels again the touch of Maya's fingers, which have shed their skin to become all bone and bark.

And those hands are around her waist now, they make burning prints on the dip between buttock and spine. Maya's liquorice voice is saying she only wanted to help. Hannah tries to hold herself back. Maya leans forward and kisses Hannah on the cheek, the fleeting touch of a feline as it slips away into the night after you've fed it. 'Don't be cross with me, Hannah, we were getting on so well, don't spoil things.'

Hannah lets herself be drawn forwards, so that her forehead touches Maya's cool one. 'Do you love me?'

'Of course I do.' Maya steps away.

'Will you be back?'

'Yeah, mebbe.'

****

Aurora has kept her vigil all the day long, gently administering water, milk and medicinal syrups when she could. The fever has finally relinquished its hold; Oliver lies peacefully in her arms. She pushes a strand of hair back from his sticky forehead.

'Once upon our time in a land very much like our own, there lived a king and queen and a princess named Aurora. Aurora had been born under a benevolent and calm sky. She had been treasured through childhood and into adolescence, shown an abundance of affection and loving guidance. Why, then, was she sitting alone in the garden at one o'clock in the morning, bemoaning her plight?

'It was two months before her sixteenth birthday and this had become an almost nightly ritual. She was dressed in the tight trousers, sweatshirt and leather jacket her mother had tried to dissuade her from buying. She had painted her nails, cut her dark hair close to her skull and, because of the cold, was wearing a shapeless knitted black hat which her mother had frequently tried to throw out. At her throat was a large, heavy, silver-coloured crucifix. Gone were the pinks and frills of girlhood or even the jeans and shirts of her early teens. It's a phase, her parents told themselves; she will grow out of it and become their own little girl again. As indeed she will.

'However, at this moment, she was sitting on the rockery smoking a cigarette bought singly at the corner shop near the school and drinking a miniature spirit bottle she had pilfered from the offie. It was, as things go, a minor rebellion. She asked herself, "Why?" Why had she ever been born? Everything seemed such a waste of time: school, homework, exams, even the holidays and trips her parents organised for her. They were a rehearsal, not the real thing, and yet she could not imagine what they were preparing her for. She dreaded that perhaps they were only the preamble to a life like her parents', dogged, structured and oh so predictable. She rested her head against the rough wood. Through the bare branches she could see the cloudy sky, grey on black. A white slither of moon was snagged in next door's hedge. Tonight was the night some called Halloween, others All Saints' Eve and still others Samhain — the start of a new year. The princess of new dawns had chosen the night of rebirths to sit and smoke a cigarette on the rockery.

'She was blithely unaware as she took another drag that the skin between her world and that of the spirits was wearing thin. If she had looked with real concentration she might have seen wraiths, their spread hands and faces pressed up against the opaque border until it de-solidified and they could melt through it. She might have heard the bridge-keeping trolls demanding their tolls, the hiss of souls searching out a new lodging. Her shiver meant she almost certainly felt the touch of a phantasm as it picked its way across her legs; its slightly acrid smell made her think of the creosote her father had painted the shed with. Her sudden unbending and stretching, which brought her to her feet, caused spectres to lose their footing and tear their gowns, which were left on the hedges and tree branches like a white mist until morning.'

Oliver's eyes open and he gurgles happily on seeing Aurora. His irises are taking on her tawny tint. 'He has your eyes,' her mother has told her. And Aurora has to agree. Her eyes in Max's face atop a little bruiser of a body. She holds out her finger and Oliver grabs hold of it. She tells him quietly, 'As the princess stepped off the rockery she almost trampled on a frog which was sitting staring at the night's visitations. It was too petrified to move and gulped two or three times as a booted foot almost squashed it. Aurora instinctively bent down to see if there was any damage done. It was a small frog which could have sat comfortably in the centre of her palm. Its wrinkled skin was so dark it was difficult to make out its patches of green. It stared up at the face staring down. It would have belched up a gold ring, or coin, or even a diamond if it could, for an apparition so beautiful. Only it could not, as it was only a common-or-garden frog. Still, it followed Aurora to the patio and watched her as she entered the house and gazed at her through the glass in the back door until she became merely a black shadow in a darkened room.'

How could she have called the police in? Max, her Max, couldn't have killed anyone. And yet he was gone for all that time and he won't account for it. She grabs up her mobile and dials his number, it goes to voicemail, she leaves a nervy message: 'Please tell the police, whatever it is that happened, please come home, we miss you, Oli and me.'

Chapter 27

Her bed has become a cave in a treacherous landscape. She buries herself in it because doing anything else would be ruinous. 'He doesn't want you, you're a nutter,' Ben's message to her plays on in her head. She'd tried so hard to act within the acceptable social norms, but he had seen through to her damaged, her unacceptable, her rotten core. Probably she is deluding herself that others are not as aware of what she's hiding. She feels so raw, she cannot bring herself out into the glare, risk them seeing it all, even being contaminated by her. She inters herself back under the covers.

Date: 09/06/09 23:11

This message will be sent via
LawrenceFielding@LawrenceFielding.co.uk
To: BenedickCartwright@therapy.co.uk
Subject: Hannah
Dear Ben,
I'm compelled to write to you to ask for your help. I am very concerned about Hannah. I haven't been able to raise her by mobile, landline or email. Have you seen her? It's not like her to be out of contact like this.
Yours, Lawrence.

Hannah makes a foray into the kitchen under the cover of darkness. There's two wine glasses — one with a smear of cherry lipstick on its rim — and some side plates with half-chewed sandwiches growing stale on the marbley cabinet tops. She wonders who has been using her parents' kitchen to feed themselves. She tells herself she must eat something healthy and discovers an apple, its skin beginning to wrinkle, in the fruit bowl. She finds a paring knife by the sink. She hesitates. Touching it could be difficult, even though she has her razor blades safely tucked away upstairs in a drawer and she no longer uses domestic cutlery. Instead she takes the apple and bites into it. It has no flavour. It's like flour paste in her mouth. She almost

172

chokes. She manages to swallow down what's in her mouth. She goes to the French windows, pulls them open and throws out the rest of the apple. A fine rain cools her cheeks, the air smells of damp seaweed, she stands out in it until she's shivering, then she scampers back to her room.

Date: 10/06/09 11:30
This message will be sent via BenedickCartwright@therapy.co.uk
To: LawrenceFielding@LawrenceFielding.co.uk
Subject: Re: Hannah
Dear Lawrence,
I haven't seen or heard from Hannah for about a week. A friend of mine, Maya Short, was with her at the weekend apparently. According to Maya, Hannah has said she doesn't want to see me again. I am a little unclear why, though there was some awkwardness between us, she seemed fine on parting and text me last week to suggest meeting again. However, I have to respect her wishes that I stay away.
All the best, Ben

Date: 10/06/09 13:12
This message will be sent via
LawrenceFielding@LawrenceFielding.co.uk
To: BenedickCartwright@therapy.co.uk
Subject: Re: Hannah
Maya, yes that was who she saw at the weekend. She's a friend of yours? Hannah seemed to be saying that there'd been some trouble between them. I got the impression Hannah was feeling very wounded. I am sure she would want to see you again. Couldn't you pop round? I'd be very grateful.
Yours, Lawrence.

Now it's black all around Hannah and she's retreated into a shed which is half-tumbling down. A man comes in. She can't see his face. He grabs her by the throat and forces something metallic-tasting down it. She knows her father is close by and tries to get him to rescue her. She screams. No-one comes. She takes up a piece of wood and smashes it into the side of her assailant's head. The plank turns into a hammer. The head turns into Dr Greene's face. The incoherent yell which bursts through her chest wakes her. The bed is no longer a place of safety. She gets up. It is light in the room, stifling, she pulls up a blind, the drab clouds are exfoliating against the window, depositing droplets of water. The cries of gulls are spectres in the gloom.

A bar or two of a Mozart concerto plays, getting louder until she remembers what it is. She finds her mobile under her jeans on the floor. She has nine messages. This last one is from Clarke, asking her where she is and why she is copping out of the course. There's one from Agatha: 'Do come back dear.' One from James, asking why she has dumped him. One from Fred, saying she's jeopardising her place on the course and will have to make the hours up. The rest are from Lawrence, getting terser as they go, the last one commanding, 'Get in touch Hannah.' She turns off her phone and hides it back in the pile of clothes. There really is no place else for her to go, except her bed. She won't sleep. She's slept too much already. But if she lies absolutely still then at least she won't shatter the fragile dome of the grieving world.

Date: 11/06/09 11:30
This message will be sent via BenedickCartwright@therapy.co.uk
To: LawrenceFielding@LawrenceFielding.co.uk
Subject: Re: Hannah
Dear Lawrence
I've known Maya since we were children. She can be a bit immature, but she has a good heart. I'm sure she wouldn't hurt Hannah, not knowingly. Perhaps there was some misunderstanding between them.
I really can't go where I'm not wanted. Hannah has others around her (on her course for instance). I am sure they will be in contact with her.
All the best, Ben.

She turns on her phone to find out what day it is. Thursday, midday. Can it really be four days since Maya left? Four days since she last spoke to another human being? She needs a shower. She reeks and her hair is greasy wire. She finds another text from Fred, giving her the deadline of this morning to let him know what is happening. *Oh well, that's that, then.* Lawrence has once again curtly ordered her to respond. And yesterday there were two texts from Elsa. The first one reads, 'Hi Hannah, I thought we had a session today. I hope you are not unwell. I missed seeing you. Elsa.' The second one, 'Please get in touch, really worried now. E.' Hannah's legs crumble and she bumps down onto the floor. *I have forgotten my clients. Elsa. Thank the Lord Darren is on holiday. How could I? How could I let Elsa down, someone who has been so badly betrayed in the past? That's it, Hannah,* she tells herself, *you've failed again. You've ballsed up your course and you've spectacularly bombed as a therapist.* She drops her mobile and reaches towards the bottom drawer of the chest in front of her, to the little make-up pouch containing the blades. Mozart's notes floating up from beside her make her jump. She answers it: it's Orwell, she's missed her supervision as well. She tries to tell him that she's giving up, she's not cut out to be a counsellor, she's sorry.

'Stop that, Hannah,' Orwell's voice booms through her faltering one. 'Tell me what's happened.'

'I don't know.' She staggers through an explanation which includes feeling lost and panicky and hurt and forgetting her clients and Elsa's texts. ('Only two?' Winters asks. 'You're getting somewhere, then.') And Fred saying she has to leave the course.

'OK, now you're going to text Elsa, apologise, tell her you're unwell and make an appointment for the end of next week. You're going to text Fred and tell him you've been speaking to me and you will meet him Monday. And you will come to talk to me ... let's see ...' He pauses and then gives her a time early the next morning.

'I'm not sure, I don't know, Orwell.' But he merely says, 'See you then,' before ringing off. She listens to the broken connection until she realises she is unbearably weary. She lies down on the carpet, curls up and closes her eyes, immediately drifting into sleep.

Date: 11/06/09 19:30
This message will be sent via TheoAkande2@yahoo.com
To: LawrenceFielding@LawrenceFielding.co.uk
Subject: Get in touch!
Hi Lawrence,
I think we need to talk, face-to-face. I need to know that you're committed to this relationship. I need to see it in your eyes.
Let me know when you'll be here. And no excuses this time.
Love Theo x

Chapter 28

The sergeants' alcove is demarcated by a partial glass partition which in reality offers no privacy. Theo imagines everyone in the incident room must see his disappointment as he puts his phone away and must know it is because his lover has failed to respond to his ultimatum. He must focus on the case, his work, his salvation. He looks up and watches Harry in a neat dark trouser suit manoeuvre around the desks — obviously making a detour to avoid three of them; he must ask her about that — to finally reach him with a cup of cappuccino and a date slice. She deposits them with a cheery, 'Elevenses Sarge.' She sits down opposite him. 'So what was Max Harris thinking of?'

What indeed? 'He says he didn't want to blow his ex-girlfriend's cover: a small town, he was worried that her new location would get back to her violent partner.' Theo takes a fortifying sip of his drink. 'And there's some arrogance: knowing he was innocent, he did not think he had to justify his actions.' Max's tale of helping his former girlfriend move and disentangle herself from an abusive relationship has checked out and, anyway, the forensics just in exonerate him. He was never in the room with Dr Greene. About the only one of the pile of suspects who wasn't.

'I suppose he didn't expect his wife to have the reaction she did, which made it all worse.' Harry nibbles thoughtfully at her white-chocolate-chip cookie. Her hair is loose around her face, falling across her blusher-grazed cheekbones. 'So are we back with Mr Olds?'

'He's recanted on his statement; I think Reggie and a few benders have prevailed. There's no more forensic evidence linking Douglas to the murder than linking, say, Ms Poole.'

'Do you really think she could have done it?'

'She'd have had to have been wearing something to protect her clothes, an overall maybe, which she chucked somehow, but why not?'

'But why? She had less reason than Mr Olds.'

'Perhaps not, perhaps they did know each other, perhaps we need to dig further into her background than we have. Perhaps we've missed something.'

'Sarge?' Harry looks surprised.

She's right, he's letting his imagination run away with him. Or rather, he's letting his personal feelings get in the way, he is in no doubt that Lawrence has been showering Hannah with texts and emails and Theo is jealous. The phone rings on the desk. After a brief exchange Theo puts the receiver down again. Piqued by a scintilla of excitement, he turns to Harry. 'Well, we shall see; Ms Poole is waiting for us downstairs and is apparently hysterical.'

'The Lord preserve me from more unbalanced women. Mrs Harris was bad enough, led us on a right wild-goose chase,' says Harry, standing up.

These had been Theo's thoughts; on hearing them from someone else, however, he feels he should defend the maligned Hannah. 'It is only the officer on reception's opinion that she is hysterical and I don't suppose he's an expert in psychology.'

****

Hannah paces the floor of the cube with its drab lino, its scratched table and chairs and its narrow window high up in the unsettlingly stained mustard wall. She is motoring on adrenalin, has been since the chaos wrought by her parents' return last night. The arguing went on into the early hours, or at least, her father's attempts to start an argument, as her mother retreated into alcoholic oblivion. It transpired that Stan Poole had managed to offend Veronica and insult her parents over a meal out. Something Hannah might have applauded him for, if he hadn't been snarling at her. Nothing was right. The house was a tip (it wasn't: she'd done some cleaning after talking to Orwell). Things had been moved in his office (they hadn't). In the end it was even her fault that he hadn't kept his temper with his daughter-in-law and her relations. But worse was to come.

She had left him to it and had gone to her room, was soothing herself by listening to her iPod, when her father banged his way in without knocking. Her yell of, 'Get the fuck out of here!' was squashed by the look of him. She hadn't noticed, he had lost weight, his bones were sticking out at the collar of his worn shirt. His hair had gone from grey to a platinum white. And his skin: his skin was yellow. She stood up and backed herself against the wall by her bed. 'Don't you touch me.' For he seemed to be coming towards her with his arms spread for an embrace. Instead he flopped down onto the corner of the bed and bent double with his face in his hands. She could see his shoulder blades like stunted wings through the faded polycotton. She couldn't move, didn't want to, was scared to. He finally spoke, words rasping out of his throat. 'I'm dying, Hannah, you have to look after me.' The sentence settled itself unpleasantly into the lining of her gut, began to gnaw away from it. He looked up at her, beseechingly. *What? What? What do you want?* her mind screamed. What came out of her mouth were questions, which he slowly and deliberately answered. Cancer. Of the bowel, of the stomach, going to his lungs. Taking him over. Inoperable. Palliative care. 'I need you, Hannah, need you to look after me.' She felt nothing but revulsion at this small goblin of a man: and anger, when had he ever looked after her? Yet, she went over to him and stroked his silky hair and patted his bony shoulders. Of course she will, of course she's here for him. It took some persuading for him to shuffle out and go to his own room. She collapsed on her bed and swallowed the screams, the sobs, retching dry tears onto her pillow.

At some point she must have slept, because she woke up. In her nightmares she had been pursued, gagged, tied, Dr Greene laughing into her face. She looked at her alarm clock. She had forty-five minutes to get to her appointment with Orwell. He listened to her talk: about Ben — 'What a fool I've been'; about Maya — 'What a complete idiot I was'; about her father — 'I can't abandon him, I'm his daughter'; and about how she's failed on her course and with her clients — 'I don't deserve to ever accredit'. He sighed and gave her a rueful smile. 'If you could stop castigating yourself for one minute, Hannah, and listen to another perspective. This is not the place to talk about Ben or Maya or your father and your responsibilities there; however, I would say relationships are made by two people, not one, and you cannot be solely accountable in any of these situations. The others have their part to play. Consider this with your therapist. As for your course and your clients, you've messed up, we all mess up. It's what actions we take when we do which are important. Do we run away, or do we face what we have done?'

'I've already got my track shoes on.'

'Not this time, Hannah; you're going to stick it out this time because one day you'll make a fine therapist.'

They had agreed on a plan of action and she had been leaving when a tall slim woman with shoulder-length brown hair and large dark eyes came up the stairs. Orwell seemed momentarily nonplussed. 'Penny,' he stumbled over the name, 'I wasn't expecting you.'

'It all happened so quickly,' Hannah explains, seated at the scarred table, Theo and Harry opposite her, their expressions bland, only their eyes are carefully scrutinising her. She feels hot. 'The woman said she had to see Orwell and he ushered her in. I'd heard Penny speak at Dr Greene's commemoration. It didn't sound like her, too high-pitched. And, I didn't think about it until afterwards, her bag: her bag was all wrong. Penny has an orange Gucci tote. She would never have gone out with that brown cracked leatherette thing. And those sandals. Don't you see?' They don't. 'It wasn't Penny, it was Eve.'

****

Theo had not seen photos of Penny and Eve side by side. Indeed he had only seen a photo of Eve which was blurry and out-of-date. Hannah had said there'd been a more recent one at the commemoration for Dr Greene, and Fred Gough (after making sure Theo knew what an inconvenience it was to him) had sent through the two he had (apparently provided by a colleague who had taken them at Eve and Dr Greene's 'wedding' party). Penny and Eve, Eve and Penny; Theo mixed up the photos and could hardly tell them apart. Even the floaty chiffon dresses were similar. He had wanted to know what alibi Penny had provided. Harry had checked it: Penny had been at some kind of poetry group; the chair, Felix Hodcroft, had identified her from a photo. 'Show him one of Eve and see what he says,' Theo had instructed. It was evening before Harry had returned with the response. Mr Hodcroft could no longer be certain it was Penny Greene he had met that afternoon. And the forensics showed Penny's fingerprints all over the room where Dr Greene had been murdered.

Darkness falls with the rain. The droplets are sharp as arrows against the windscreen. The harbour is drowning amongst the lead waves. The sea is grabbing back the land. Water is sinking all puny human endeavour. Theo shivers. It is not a night to be out on the roads, though he feels safe with Harry at the wheel. Nor is it a night for moving house. Yet as they approach the Esplanade flat which once belonged to Dr Greene and where Penny has been residing, Theo can see a van being loaded by two scurrying figures, twins in their long hooded macs. The buildings here are tall, elegant, with balconies, many adorned with hanging baskets, looking out over the bay. Generously proportioned, broad-doored and with bay windows, the one thing which is small in these apartments is the lift, which approximates a gilded upright coffin. If this were not so, and they hadn't had to struggle with various boxes and bits of furniture down the stairs, Eve and Penny might well have already flown. They would have been on their way to the ferry which would eventually take them to the house they'd just purchased in France. Instead, Theo takes them silent and dripping to the police station.

They are good — Penny and Eve, Eve and Penny, a slick double act — well rehearsed and sticking to their stories. Having spoken to both of them during the gloomy hours as the rain pitted itself against the glass panes, Theo suspects Penny is the one who is orchestrating it all. She is the more self-assured, the more relaxed on being interrogated. He thinks maybe he could trip up Eve if he were given time, but as Reggie's soberly dressed female colleague (who takes over from the duty officer in the morning) points out, there is nothing to link Eve to the murder scene. Indeed she has evidence (rail tickets conveniently still in her purse) to say she arrived in Scarborough a few days ago. Penny has always said she visited Dr Greene's therapy room before Douglas Olds came in, to inspect the new decor, which would explain the forensics. If only one of her fingerprints had been bloody. But she's too clever for that. Theo can see her shrewdness deep in the fathoms of her large jet eyes. There's only one moment when he senses a slight fissure in the steel plating, when he mentions Douglas Olds, the possibility of him taking the rap. Then she's reinforced again, declaring, if he's innocent, the British justice system will keep him safe. Theo knows he has lost; he says with an edge of spite, 'Isn't it unusual for a current partner to be friends with, to choose to live with, an ex-one?'.

Penny smiles at him; she must be tired (he is) yet she maintains a stoic good humour. 'Unusual; however, not criminal, I believe. Remember I knew Eve before I knew Themis, I met her through a pottery class we both attended. It was never my intention to hurt her.'

'And Dr Greene? Did you always intend to hurt her? To pay her back for what she did to Eve?'

She briefly lifts her eyebrows. 'My goodness, Sergeant Akande,' (how carefully she pronounces his name) 'what an imagination. Eve and I lost touch; it was only recently, when she heard about my troubles, that she got in touch again. I know I should have told you, but there's no way she could have been involved, she was at the other end of the country and she's been such a support since Themis died.'

'So much so you've bought a place together, in France?'

'Eve has always wanted to go and settle over there, establish herself as a ceramics artist. She really is very good, you know. She had her eye on a place, and with selling the flat here and the Jersey house, we've been able to make it happen. I wouldn't have wanted to stay here or go back to Jersey, not without Themis.'

Theo wonders what she called Dr Greene when they were alone together: *surely not 'Them'? Perhaps she knows she was really 'Thelma'?* 'How neat and convenient,' he says.

'There's been nothing neat or convenient about having my life partner murdered, Sergeant Akande,' she replies, her voice heavy with upset. Theo almost believes her.

Eve is altogether more easily rattled. She admits using her middle name and her mother's maiden name to 'hide out', 'give her some space', 'to recover'. She perhaps strays from the agreed narrative when she admits calling Aurora because she wanted to hear news about 'my boys' and contacting Orwell for the same reason. 'I've known Orwell since I was a little girl, Sergeant.' (She is unable to say his name or even look him in the face.) 'His dad would bring him to the farm secretly so his mum didn't know.' Then she adds quickly, 'But I only got in contact with him just now, I mean.' She hesitates before saying with uncertainty, 'Yesterday.'

Penny and Eve, Eve and Penny, a slick double act. As dawn liquefies into a grey morning, Theo lets them go, with a warning to stay put in Scarborough: he may want to talk to them again. He sends Harry home and returns to his own, planning to sleep until lunchtime and then return to work. It's 10:30am when his phone's melodic ringtone wakes him.

Chapter 29

Theo is furious. The DI is implacable. 'It's a result, Detective Sergeant, and that's all we need.' He drops his gaze to some reports he has on his desk. Theo is dismissed. He strides out. A young girl, a temp, sits at Suze's desk; she crouches over her keyboard, not able to meet the anger he's flinging out around him. Suze is having one of her 'off weeks', unable to get into work. For a moment he takes it as a personal insult that she is not available to him. Harry is also unaccountably absent. Theo stomps down the stairs and out into the damp air. He doesn't stop. He is almost halfway there before he realises that he is on his way to see Orwell and should have brought his jacket: he is chilly.

Orwell's, 'I can only spare you twenty minutes' infuriates Theo further.

'A woman has been murdered and a man has committed suicide, Mr Winters. Doesn't that bother you in the least bit?'

The news had obviously reached Orwell, he is calm in his reply, 'I do not take responsibility for either death. I did not kill Thelma Green. Both Hannah Poole and I reported Mr Olds as a suicide risk. The inadequacies of the crisis mental health services in this area are down to the government, not me. I do not rejoice at anyone taking their own life; however, Douglas had plenty of his own demons.'

The reports are only just coming in and being handled by a specialist in child abuse from York, what did Orwell know and how? 'What do you mean?'

'My daughters were at the school he taught at, I helped a friend of theirs make a complaint. He was not believed, of course. Kids never were in those days. I hope there will be a better reception this time around.'

'So Mr Olds is a convenient fall guy in your little scheme?'

'Sergeant Akande, I have no little scheme.'

'You knew Eve was here in Scarborough; you met with her.'

Orwell's face is mask-like. 'I met with Penny. I have not seen Eve since her and Thelma's so-called wedding.'

'Except that's a lie, like saying you didn't know her when you were children.' Orwell does not react. The DI has made it clear Theo will get no more funding to check further into Eve's movements. Theo continues in a metallic tone: 'Child abuse, however horrific it might be, does not carry a death sentence in this country. Nor does murder.'

Pause. The older man says in quiet, measured tones, 'In my younger days I was fervently against the death penalty, these days I wonder if a death sentence is worse than a life sentence.'

'I am not here to discuss the niceties of the penal system; the point is, you do not have the authority to bestow a sentence of any kind.'

'I did not.' His face is as grey as his beard, his lips dry. 'If you want to talk about someone misusing authority, let's talk about Thelma Green, without a PhD and without an "e". Leaving aside what she did to Eve, for a moment, only a very bad or negligent therapist would have missed Douglas Olds' disposition and Thelma was very able, very able indeed. She must have known and she had a duty to take some action. Only she didn't. Why? Because it suited her to carry on with Douglas to prove her point, that her particular approach to therapy could cure sex offenders, which just happened to be the subject of the book she was working on when she died.'

'You didn't act either.'

'I tried, all those years ago. I didn't even know Mr Olds was Thelma's client until this ... this recent episode. If Thelma had just once done what was morally and ethically fitting, instead of what served her best interests, then we might well not be in this situation now. You are correct, Sergeant: two people are dead. In addition, two local lads grew up without their mum, a fragile young woman was used abominably, some very damaged young men will never see their abuser brought to justice, I am back in therapy and a promising counsellor is becoming more troubled by the day. I'm not sure I can work out how the scales are tilting in terms of rights and wrongs, can you?'

'I could have you for perverting the course of justice,' Theo growls. He feels the energy running out of him. Orwell shrugs. He appears unconcerned and he's probably right to be: even if Theo could make it stick, what would be the point? Orwell looks at his watch. Theo doesn't argue. He wants out of here. He wants done with the case of Dr Thelma Greene. As he steps into a dim, steamy sunshine, he imagines two women who could pass for twins quietly running a B&B which offers ceramics courses, somewhere near Menton, the love of one healing the wounds of the other, and two motherless boys finding they have options beyond the farm they grew up on because of a surprise anonymous windfall. And he wonders if the scales are creaking back towards an equilibrium.

Chapter 30

By the time a citrus sun finally drips languorously through the clouds onto the damp lawn it is evening time. At least it would be if it weren't the longest day, and dusk is still some hours off. Aurora has showered, she and her mother have given each other a manicure and an elegantly twisted henna bracelet, a skill learnt on trips to her father's family. Now she is dressing in her black linen trousers (with the forgiving tied waist) and a pale-jade silk blouse. Rose had specified a light colour should be worn and green seemed to fit the season. Aurora inspects herself in the mirror; it feels like the first time she has seen herself properly since, well, since before the birth. Her reflection has substance, she can connect herself to it, she can even be relatively pleased with it. Her parents had arrived and she had wept for an hour in her mother's arms, while her father had quietly tended to Oliver. She had been relieved to relinquish control to them, though also glad to regain some of it as the week went on. Her mother had gone to Dr Courtney's with her and they had returned with some antidepressants, which she had dutifully begun to take. She was told it would be three weeks before they had any effect, but she is already feeling more grounded and together. She is sure it isn't all chemically induced. It's been crucial for her to be cosseted and surrounded by her parents' emotional support. 'You're doing fine, Aurora, you don't have to be perfect.' 'You were, Mum.' 'No I wasn't, darling, I was good enough.' Not to mention their practical attention. Yet the change had started before they came: she has the impression it began when she had told Oliver a fairy story.

She finds her mint-coloured wrap because Rose had said they would be outside and goes to say farewell to her sleeping son and to her parents, who will babysit while she is gone. I should only be a couple of hours, she tells them; they say (as they always have), take as long as you wish. She shuts the front door and realises it is only the second time she has left the house without a baby (the first time being earlier this week to visit the GP). She feels his absence, misses his sticky grip on her finger, his

187

gurgling, his eyes watching her, searching. For what? Love, she supposes. She prays (to any god who might be listening) she has enough to give him. Once she is down the path and through the gate, she has more of a sense of freedom. She is out on her own. Aurora. She is merely herself. Not a pregnant woman, a new mum, a failing mum, a single mum. Her thoughts stray to the phone call she and Max had during the afternoon. They had both cried. She can't remember ever hearing him in tears before. The sobs were those of the unaccustomed, they tore at her heart. 'I'm sorry, I'm sorry, Aurora, please.' It was easy to forgive him. Could he forgive her? He had said yes. She hopes they can both keep to their undertakings.

Aurora had been shocked on visiting Hannah earlier in the week to find her bleary-eyed and dishevelled, speaking in a dull monotone. She had persuaded her to accept Rose's invitation to come and celebrate midsummer with her. Tonight Hannah is (at least) washed and dressed in jeans and white cotton blouse, her glossy mahogany hair curling to her shoulders. She has some mascara on and a touch of silvery eyeshadow; she has a white-stoned ring on her dainty ring finger. Her hazel eyes are large in her wan face and Aurora thinks she might have lost weight. However, she is up and ready, only mithering for a moment over where her keys are when they are already in her bag. The drive over to Rose's village is uneventful. They listen to some comedy on the radio, the two of them relaxing as they laugh.

Rose lives in one of a terrace of what must have been some farm labourer cottages built of stone and slate. Some have been extended on or up. Rose's, near the top end where the road runs into a dirt track bounded by fields, is unaltered, its lintel above its low door slightly askew. Rose, dressed in a long, white, heavily brocaded dress, her grey hair twisted up into a bun, ushers them in with welcoming hellos. They enter a small porch and then the living room with stairs going to the upper floors, and through that they go to the kitchen, where Rose offers them some sweet home-made elderflower champagne. It is the first alcohol Aurora has drunk for over a year; she feels mellow, slightly giggly. In the fuchsia- and cherry-painted lounge, they toast the summer, which appears to have taken its own holiday. Hannah picks up a photo of a grinning teenager in a skimpy bikini on a tropical beach seated by a tanned, handsome, mature man who has his arm around the slender girl's shoulders. Despite the petiteness of the girl and the rhobustness of Rose, Aurora is not surprised to learn the photo is of the older woman's daughter. 'With her father,' is added as an afterthought.

'She does have one, then?' Hannah says, surprising Aurora with her causticity.

'Of course.' There's a slight tension in Rose's voice. 'She's gone to him today, Ben told me. She's been staying with him in town.' There's a sadness in her tone which makes Aurora uneasy, as she is unused to it in Rose. Hannah is still studying the photo, so Aurora takes over the questioning. Rose obliges with answers: after growing up in Scarborough, sometimes living with her aunt, whose house she's inherited and they are now sitting in, Rose went to London to train as a nurse, enjoying the sixties lifestyle to the full, by her own account. She then joined Médcins Sans Frontières and met Serge Girouette, a French doctor, who was already married with children. They had an on-off affair for some eight years, dependent on where they were posted, until Rose got pregnant and came back to her late aunt's home to have her baby. She was thirty-eight.

Aurora looks round the room, making sense of the brightly hued rugs, beaten metal plates and landscape photos which adorn it. 'Did you think — I mean were you hoping ...?

'He'd leave his wife for me?' She shrugs her round shoulders. 'I was silly and was quite unworldly in some ways, despite my physical age and experiences. I had a lot of growing-up to do.'

'Yet she sees him — your daughter, I mean?'

'It's always been like that. He sent me money regularly and as soon as was practical Maya would spend time with him and his family.'

'How extraordinary.'

Hannah breaks in: 'She's been staying with Ben? Ben told you? You've spoken to Ben? Today?'

'Yes, he phoned, said he wouldn't be coming tonight. And told me about Maya.'

'He might have been here?' Aurora can't tell if it is panic or excitement that is animating Hannah's features.

'We usually see the seasons turn together,' Rose says, a slight frown appearing between her thick, salt-lined brows. She thoughtfully regards the other woman for a moment.

Hannah puts down the photo carefully where she found it. 'Wouldn't you have preferred to hear from Maya herself that she was leaving?'

'Maya ...' Rose snaps, before pausing and then carrying on more moderately. 'My daughter is her own woman now, and I'm glad of it.' She falters slightly. 'It couldn't have been easy for her being brought up by a single mum, especially one like me, not terribly maternal.'

'Oh no, Rose.' Aurora is light-headed from finishing off her glass; she doesn't want to hear about another woman's fears of being a bad mum. 'I'm sure you were a wonderful mother.'

Rose smiles grimly. 'I'm sure I was not. I learnt on the job. Maybe we all do.' Then she levers herself up. 'Shall we go?'

They dutifully follow her out through the kitchen, out the back door and along a path to a fairly substantial garden shed. Inside, the wooden walls are covered by dark velvet, the small windows by dark opaque fabric. There is a subdued light produced by a fat golden wax candle hanging in each corner and there are bunches of lavender and lilac, along with sprigs of oak leaves, in a half-keg which sits in the centre of the floor. The heavy, syrupy scents mingle with that of some spicy incense. Rose invites them to sit in a circle around the keg. She explains this is a sacred space, the candles are lit at the portals of the four quarters, North, South, East and West (she points out each direction as she says it). It is midsummer day, the longest day, the day when the sun is at its zenith. His power is at its peak and will decline from this time onwards. She smiles at Hannah. 'It is also a special day for you: you were birthed at midsummer, a sun baby.' Aurora is about to exclaim that if she'd known she'd have brought a card, only Rose's expression discourages it. She then turns to Aurora. 'And you are a moon child, a midwinter's day baby.' She looks from one to the other. 'Two halves of the turning year here with me tonight.' Aurora doesn't bother to enquire how Rose knows, she accepts that she just does.

Rose suggests they are quiet for a while, close their eyes, focus on their breath, letting thoughts slip through their minds unattended to. Aurora tries to do as she is bid, though unwanted doubts about how Oliver might be, how her parents are coping, what will happen when she sees Max again, they all come and won't leave so easily. And she realises too late that she should have gone to the toilet before coming over here. Rose speaks again, she's inviting the spirits of the earth, the spirits of the air, of water, of fire to be with them. 'We are mindful of your powers; earth that both nurtures and provides can also erupt, causing devastation. Earth, teach us how to create a nourishing, secure home. Air, from the soft breezes which cool us, to the tempests, assist us to be astute in our thoughts. Fire, the hearth fire which keeps us warm, the raging fire that consumes, teach us to be true to our passions and yet not be slaves to them. And Water, the soothing spring, the wild sea, bring us compassion for our fellow beings who we build our lives amongst. Mother Moon, father Sun, join us on this your auspicious day. Bring us your gifts.'

There is stillness. Aurora finds her fingertips are tingling; maybe it is because she is gripping her hands together. She feels calm, sleepy almost: the effect of the champagne? Rose explains that the moon's face is hidden, it is the dark moon, the wise old crone. 'Ask her for her wisdom. Ask the sun for his element, his fire, his passion, his guidance in worldly affairs. Ask them for their blessings on us and on those who love us and those who love us not, indeed know us not.' Again there is hush. Aurora asks silently that she and Max may find their way to being back together once more. Finally Rose offers round a goblet of bramble wine, they take sips for themselves and pour an offering into a metallic bowl for the spirits who gather about them. They stand and, linking hands, walk slowly clockwise round the keg. 'So we symbolise the turning of the year; as day follows day and season season, we also will have our seasons, our moments when we are as bright and fiery as midsummer and our moments when we are as dark and closed in as midwinter. Each has its purpose, welcome each, honour each. Our seasons will turn and a new day will dawn.'

They hug and kiss, Rose and Aurora with some fervour, Hannah more awkwardly. They extinguish the candles and walk back to the house. A deep-purple evening littered with stars encroaches on the thick foliage — beans, cabbages, rhubarb, raspberries in their fecund rows. Aurora looks back and sees what is, after all, only a shed at the end of the garden.

There is coffee and fresh strawberries dipped in bitter chocolate as Rose and Aurora encourage the reluctant Hannah to say what's ailing her. 'I'm tired,' she offers and Aurora commiserates with the effects of lack of profound sleep. They do not stay much longer as Aurora is keen to get back now to see Oliver. 'What do you think of that?' she asks in the car.

'Not much.'

'I found it peaceful. I feel,' she searches for the word, 'settled.'

'Do you?' Hannah stares out of the side window, discouraging further discussion.

When they arrive back, Hannah exits the car slowly and stops on the pavement outside the car. Aurora feels the tug to invite her in. She resists, she wants to be with her little family; and finally the other woman walks reluctantly away.

Chapter 31

Theo has taken a week off. 'I hope you are not reconsidering your position here with us,' Hoyle had said. 'You know how we value you.' (*Yeah for increasing your percentage of officers from minority backgrounds,* Theo had thought, a smile nevertheless engraved on his face.) He has slept in late and breakfasted slowly on real coffee, tangy blackcurrants (from Suze's garden) and warm croissants. Now he is staring at the unpacked boxes in his spare room. Should he make a start on them? Should he leave them? He is still prevaricating when the doorbell goes. Expecting the postie, he is hardly looking as he opens the door and barely registers who it is for a second. When he does, he wants to shout, he wants to grin. 'Lawrence.'

'I hope this is not inconvenient.' He is smartly dressed in a coal-coloured wool jacket and damson scarf; he is carrying a leather holdall. He's too tall for the doorway and is stooping slightly, his grey hair flopping into his blue eyes.

Theo shakes his head, not moving aside.

'Can I come in, then? Or must a man declare his heart's desire in the street?'

Once inside, it takes a while for Lawrence to declare anything; perhaps this is because Theo insists on plying him with food and drink and on showing him around the house. After this frenetic energy has been spent and has pulled them through the awkwardness, Lawrence suggests they sit on the sofa. 'I'm sorry I didn't reply to your email. I wanted to be sure. I've not felt this way before and … ' His face is grave, his tone gruff; he looks at Theo and then glances down at his large, fidgeting hands.

Theo reaches out to still those fingers with his own. 'You don't have to say …'

'I do. I do.' His features are sad. 'You're right, I've been non-committal, I guess it's because I didn't expect you to want to be with me. On past experience, people, men haven't …'

'I do.'

A grimace., 'I don't know why.'

'I don't either.' They both laugh. It's easier after that to give and receive apologies, reassurances, promises. Lawrence will stay a few days, and — he produces a key — this is for Theo, for the house in London. Theo takes it: it feels warm. It is only later that he asks about Hannah.

'She doesn't know I'm here. Well, I didn't know I was coming until this morning when I sat down to write to you and thought what I really want is to see you, be with you.'

'You going to call her?' Theo keeps his tone casual.

Lawrence gives the glass of wine he is holding his consideration, then says, 'No, this is for us, isn't it?'

At last the pressure at the top of Theo's spine eases and the apprehension rolls away.

****

At last it feels like it's all been said. Explanations, regrets, words of contrition. She and Max have been round it all a number of times. He has bought her flowers and moved back in. Her parents have left and she has cooked him dinner. And they are bordering on their first argument: can't he stop looking at his work emails for a single moment? Doesn't he notice the tidying which needs doing? Can't she let Oli sniffle for a second? Does she always have to leap up the moment he starts? Aurora bites back her snappy reply and sits on the couch beside him, laying her head on his shoulder. He closes down his laptop and puts his arm around her shoulder. She tells him she's anxious about Hannah and the scratches on her arm. 'Are you, love?' He kisses the top of her head. 'You worry too much. I'm sure she'll be okay. Everything's going to be great from now on, you'll see.'

****

Hannah has held it together for a week. She has been to her course, seen Elsa, been to her placement, even managed a tolerably civilised conversation with her parents about her father's future care. She has not tried to contact Ben, has forced herself not to think of him more than maybe three times each day. She has read in the local paper that Douglas Olds has committed suicide just as the police were about to charge him for Dr Themis Greene's murder. It has helped to recall midsummer with Rose and Aurora. Then for a moment she had felt peace. Into the quiet, she had heard the rustle of a fox passing by outside through the undergrowth. She had felt a silver glow pour over her, a fountain of warm energy, and she had heard the words as the music of flowing water: 'All will be well and all will be well, Hannah. Don't give up on yourself, and all will be well.'

It has all been possible to contain, until this moment.

This moment in this lavender-hued room, the whole edifice splinters and begins to fall about her, glass fragments plummet, daggers cutting through the air, missing her by inches. If she could scream she would. If she could run, she would. She has to stay very still to prevent the world coming to an end.

'Tell me what's going on, Hannah,' Izzie asks gently for the second time, leaning forward.

If she could give an explanation, she would. She tries to open her mouth. Finally prising her jaws apart, the words tumble out. 'I was there, then they died. I killed them. And it's happening all over again.' An unearthly wail emanates from somewhere uncharted within her. Hannah folds in on herself, at last accepting the embrace of her therapist's arms.

Thank you

Thank you to you the reader for spending time with my story. If you have any comments, please send them to AvenuePressScarb@talktalk.net.

Thank you to all those who supported me in this endeavour, gave me advice and encouragement; especially Lesley and Ros and my many writing friends. Thank you to those who represent the very best in therapy and helped me know myself better, especially Rufus, Dan and Annie. Thank you to my husband, Mark, for his unstinting love, sustenance and backing, which has got me through the hard times and much, much more. Proofreading by Jenny Drewery, www.thewriterthebetter.co.uk. All the mistakes which remain are my own.

'The Art of the Imperfect' is the first in a series of crime novels based in Scarborough. Turn the page to read an extract from the next in the series, 'The Art of Survival', due for publication 2015.

The sea sucks in through its incisors — hesitates — then spits out the bitter brine. Hannah sinks deeper into her padded anorak, pulls her woollen hat further down over her ears and then digs her gloved hands into her pockets. The wind smells of snow. Hannah drinks it in like it's a numbing alcohol, clearing her airways of the odours she's carried from home: shit, bleach and unwashed bodies. Both of her parents appear to have given up on showers over the last several weeks. Her father drags himself from bed to commode, refusing to surrender pyjamas or dressing gown; while her mother layers on perfume and increasingly brassy make-up. Her numerous friends have turned out to be mere acquaintances and have stopped calling. The graphite waves stealthily begin to retake the pathway that encircles the old South Bay lido (filled in years ago) where Hannah stands braced against the metal railings. The concrete turns to froth, which flicks tongues of ice up the pool's crumbling wall and over the tips of Hannah's wellies. She imagines herself easing into those dark mountains and being enveloped by a watery blanket, her oxygen cut off, gently launched into her grave like some Viking princess. *Drowning happens quickly,* she tells herself, *over before you know it. Just let go. Fall. It would be easier not to exist.* Still the railings hold her back and she knows she does not have the strength to resist them. She turns abruptly and starts to walk. *I will find another way.*

As she comes down from the grassed and tarmacked lido to the path which leads along the bottom of the cliffs to the Gothic-style Victorian Spa buildings, she notices a gaunt figure standing on a concrete promontory the other side of the sea wall. She pauses, watching the hunched form advance towards the titanic waves, its (gender as yet unidentified) scrawny bare arms forming an inadequate umbrella over its head. *Another person contemplating oblivion. Good luck to them. They have grasped the truth: life isn't worth the effort.* Hannah moves on. Then she stops. Something is nagging at her brain, something along the lines of, *I'm a (not-quite-qualified) counsellor, I don't walk past someone in distress and do nothing.* The conversation in her head continues: *'So? People make choices and that person has made their choice. Who am I to interfere?' 'You're a counsellor, you have some ethical responsibilities.' 'To interfere with a person's freely taken choice?' 'How do you know it's a freely taken choice? Go back, at least find out what's going on.'* Slowly she turns and walks towards the waif in black who is now performing some kind of dance, two steps forwards, the waves crash over and she stumbles back. *Jump, you coward.* The words clatter into Hannah's brain. *Do it for me. Because I can't.*

By the time she reaches the would-be suicide a couple have arrived there first. She, with her carefully coifed blonde bob and in her smart camel-coloured coat and matching knee-length boots, is seated on the wall. Her arm is stretched out towards the person, who Hannah can now identify as a young woman, possibly in her twenties, possibly younger, skeletal, bone-white under all her black. Blonde Bob is coaxing her in, calmly but assertively. She never takes her eyes off the shivering urchin who is still tangoing with the waves. The male companion of Blonde Bob is speaking into his flash phone. *They are doing what I should have done, should be doing.* She feels awkward. She notes that she used to have as good dress sense — *didn't I?* Her hair was once that well kempt — *wasn't it?* All before she left London to come to her parents' chosen place of retirement, this last-stop-on-the-line town by the sea, some twelve months ago. She thinks of her years lodging on the top floor of her friend Lawrence's Highgate house working as copy-editor and proofreader to him and others at his publishers. She remembers it as being cosy, untroubled. *Wasn't it? Why did I leave? To finish my training as a counsellor,* she reminds herself. *To complete something for once in my life.* Then she tells herself off for wasting precious minutes. She should be in there, helping Blonde Bob, using her skills, taking charge. She sees the intimacy being built up between the woman on the wall and the youngster now being tempted from her fascination with the water. Hannah hangs back. She realises she should not intrude at this critical moment. She berates herself for not having gone forward in the first instance.

'That's it, that's it, come on over, now, that's better. You sit beside me. I like the sea too, but it's cold this time of year, isn't it?' Wet and shiny as a freshly caught eel, the young woman crouches on the sheltered side of the wall and Blonde Bob is still talking as if they had bumped into each other on a sunny summer afternoon. 'My name's Trina. What's yours?' No response. 'I'm up here for the weekend, from London. Where are you from?' No response. 'It's cold today for a swim, isn't it? How about we go for a coffee, warm up?' No response. Up close, Hannah sees the scars that ring the thin arms and even the neck. She balls her hands up in her pockets. Jealous? Could she possibly be jealous? This woman's scars are on show. The youngster's name has finally escaped from between her clattering teeth. 'Right then, Loretta,' responds Trina. 'You put your jumper and coat on and we'll go for a coffee.' Both Hannah and Trina can see what Loretta cannot as she dresses in her abandoned outer clothing, which is almost as soaked as she is — that Trina's male companion has finished his phone conversation and is jerking his head towards the town. Following his gaze, Hannah sees a police car turn off the main foreshore road and carefully pick its way along the narrow thoroughfare past the Spa towards them.

They make a strange cameo. Loretta, tall but bent over, her drenched jumper and coat hanging about her, ragged mourning weeds, stumbling between Trina (keeping up her cheerful chatter) and her bloke, dressed for a day at the races. And Hannah bringing up the rear, a disgraced terrier all too aware of its failings. They are met in front of the rows of closed-up beach huts by the police van. Hannah hangs back, maybe even now she could be of use. A rotund PC gets out and goes towards Trina and her charges. Hannah recognises the officer from another episode earlier in the year, which she would rather forget — though finding a dead body (especially if it belongs to an eminent psychotherapist you've only encountered in books before) is not so easily filed away. She searches for the PC's name; she did know it once. And beside him is Theo, *Detective Sergeant Theo Akande*, she corrects herself. She has come to know as Theo since he hooked up with Lawrence. Theo's spare frame is resolutely wrapped in his duffle coat and red scarf, his mahogany skin all the more startling in this wintry world of greys and whites. It is he who speaks to Loretta, while the PC splits off the other two to get their story. Theo bends forward to catch the young woman's words, which she lets fall to the concrete. It's moments before he is able to persuade her to the car, where there is a woman PC who guides her into the back.

Hannah turns towards the winding route which ascends between the beach huts, through the cliff gardens and onto the Esplanade. She had done nothing, nothing; she doesn't want Theo to express his disappointment to her. But she is too late, his call to her reaches her and she halts. He bounds up the rickety steps and gives her a quick hug, she can smell his warmth, could sink into it, if she could let herself. He draws back, his hands on her shoulders. His brown eyes gaze quizzically from behind their glasses. Red frames today, to go with the red scarf, which Hannah identifies as cashmere, and, therefore, almost definitely a gift from Lawrence. He asks her if she's OK, but she knows what he really wants to find out is her connection to the incident he is currently dealing with. She tells him what she witnessed, making her role sound supportive; essential, almost. 'Why'd they send a detective out on something as routine as this?'

He mutters quickly about a missing girl and Hannah remembers the news reports. A different girl. A little girl. A girl with bunches of brown hair and a blue bike with stabilisers and. A girl without scars on her arms and neck. An altogether more lovable girl. He says, 'Do you know her?'

He means through her work at the Scarborough Centre for Therapy Excellence. She shakes her head. 'Today's the first time I've seen her. By the looks of her, though, I'd say you'll find records about her in some mental health service or other.'

He nods, he glances towards the waiting police car, still he does not go. Finally he says, 'You're sure you're OK? You look ... I mean with your dad and everything ...are you OK?'

'I'm fine, yes, absolutely.' She presses her lips together.

'Well, if you're sure?' His hands have fallen to his sides, his feet have turned imperceptibly away from her.

She nods. And he hurries back down to where his job awaits him. She continues on her way, beginning to clump up the rest of the steps and onto the path, the words, *My father will be dead very soon* falling in with the rhythm of her feet.

Printed in Great Britain
by Amazon.co.uk, Ltd.,
Marston Gate.